I0522537

They weren't intimidated because she was a woman, but she would show them…

The lights went out.

"Uh!" she cried and fell back against the pile, as if hit. The glare was gone, and she couldn't see anything. Blind. In the dark. Her legs and arms trembled again. *Hurry up, Tom.*

They must turn the lights out at midnight. She fumbled around until her hand found the machete. How could she frighten anyone with it if they couldn't see it?

The low rumble of an engine stopped. She heard footsteps and voices whispering. She began to see the outline of her pile in the dim moonlight. She whirled to face the whispered comments. The bulk of four men huddled together not five meters from her. Wide awake now, she raised the machete to fight them off.

"Help! Police!" she cried in Spanish. *Maybe that policeman will hear.* "Don't come near me. I'll cut you if you try to steal my crates. Keep away. My boyfriend is coming."

The four men came closer. "Oh yeah? Where is he now?"

"Julio!"

A deep breath. Heat swarmed through her. For a long second, she didn't move. Then her sore leg muscles burst into action and crunched the gravel beneath her. She ran forward to meet them swinging her sword like an ancient warrior. They stopped, but they didn't back up. *They aren't afraid of me because I'm a woman.* She saw that two of them had machetes that they raised to bring down on her if she got too close. She turned aside, afraid, but then cried out in anger, whirled around, and slashed Julio in the leg. He screamed and waved his hand to his men. "Get her!"

Backpacking through Nicaragua with her boyfriend Tom, Jamie discovers her father has actually paid him to be her bodyguard. Furious, she wants nothing more to do with him—despite the attraction they feel for each other—but before she can storm off on her own, her uncle calls with a desperate plea for help. He's a doctor working with primitives in the Amazon jungle. He needs her to send a helicopter to rescue him before an outsider-fearing neighboring tribe kills him.

Knowing she can't pull the rescue off by herself, Jamie reluctantly forgives Tom, and he agrees to help. To get the money needed for the helicopter, she and Tom take a job delivering some heavy crates to a man on the other side of Nicaragua. However, they are not the only ones interested in the crates. Fighting off pirates and smugglers, Jamie and Tom will be lucky to survive the delivery, let alone the jungle rivers, alligators, and mosquitos. Can Tom find the courage and strength to win Jamie? Can she rescue her uncle, earn her independence, and still keep Tom?

KUDOS for *Machetes for Two*

In *Machetes for Two* by Carol J. Megge, Jamie and her boyfriend Tom are backpacking through Nicaragua when Jamie discovers that Tom was actually hired by her over-protective father as a bodyguard. Jamie is furious, but she needs Tom to help her rescue her uncle who is stranded in the Amazon jungle. In order to raise money to hire a helicopter to fly her uncle to safety, Jamie and Tom take on a dangerous delivery job, taking crates to the other side of the country. They are told there are diamond cores in the crates, but Jamie and Tom are suspicious. Still, if they want the money, they have to deliver the crates. What follows is a harrowing adventure. Fending of pirates and smugglers, as well as dangerous animals, Jamie and Tom are putting their lives on the line. And they have no guarantee they will actually get paid if they make it to where they are supposed to deliver the crates. Megge gives us an exciting adventure, full or twists and turns, vivid scenes, and intriguing characters, combined with a spicy romance. A great read. *~ Taylor Jones, The Review Team of Taylor Jones & Regan Murphy*

Machetes for Two by Carol Megge is the story of a modern woman who can take care of herself, or so she thinks. Stubborn and fiercely independent, Jamie is furious when finds out the man she has been backpacking with in South American is not really her boyfriend but a bodyguard hired by her father. Tom insists that he really cares for her, but he went along with her father because he needs the money to help his own father who has cancer. Jamie is torn between going off on her own or sticking with Tom because she cares for him too. But before she can make up her mind, she gets a phone call from her doctor uncle who needs to be rescued from the Amazon jungle, and Jamie is his last resort. Jamie knows she can't do this by herself so she agrees not go off on her own if Tom will help rescue her uncle. Because they need to hire a helicopter, they are forced to take a job delivering some crates for a shady character all the way across Nicaragua, going by van and then by boat. It is supposed to be an easy job, but they are not told about the dangers—pirates, smugglers, alligators, jaguars, and mosquitoes big enough to carry off a small car. *Machetes for Two* is a romance combined with an exciting adventure, foreign intrigue, fast-paced action, and enchanting characters, and the author's vivid descriptions make you feel like you're there. *~ Regan Murphy, The Review Team of Taylor Jones & Regan Murphy*

ACKNOWLEDGMENTS

Undying thanks to my friend, Judy Kammeraad, for her gentle but relentless critiquing of my first novel, and to Kathy Smits who did me the honor of beta-reading it.

To my editor, Faith, and to my publishers, Black Opal Books, this first novel has been an education. Thank you.

Most of all, gratitude to the Sunshine State Romance Authors for their ideas, for the teaching about character and conflict, and for their unending encouragement. Special thanks to Loretta Rogers (my first reader), and to Dylan Newton, who taught me organization. To my friends in the Florida Hysterical Writers Group, thank you for hours of patient critiquing and laughter. Good writers all.

Machetes for Two

Carol J. Megge

A Black Opal Books Publication

DEDICATION

To Ken, who first told me to write a novel.

With much love to my husband, Jerry O,
and to my two daughters, Kathy and Kris,
who always have encouraged and helped.

Chapter 1

The Call

Jamie balled her napkin, grabbed her pack, and marched out of the hostel breakfast room. She didn't care that the other backpackers in the room were staring at her. She wouldn't let Tom win this argument after lying to her all summer long. She still couldn't believe it. Her father had paid him! Well, they'd be home in two weeks, and she wouldn't have to put up with the "bodyguard" her father had chosen to "protect" her on this backpacking trip through Mexico and Nicaragua.

And the job didn't entitle him to sex.

But I've been so tempted.

Well, Tom wasn't really a bodyguard. He was only an anthropology student like her, who happened to have a lot of muscles. She had barely known him at the university, but after six weeks of spending every day together, he wanted the nights too.

He kept a secret from me. I won't make love with him now. She crumpled against the wall. *It hurts. If he's in it for the money, then our whole relationship is a lie.* She kicked the wall.

Biting her lip, she came out of the shadowy hallway into the heat of the morning sun, dumped her pack and settled on the front stoop of the Nicaraguan hostel.

Who am I kidding? I want him.

All those wonderful muscles. She wanted to lick them. She wanted to run her hands all over his skin. She wanted skin to skin that would make her let loose. Her insides tightened with that familiar ache. Her hand went out to touch the warm cement stoop that she wanted to be his warm body. He was her best friend, but he hadn't told her.

Should I trust him? If I hadn't found that agreement this morning with my father's signature I never would have known.

The door opened behind her, and Tom's hand landed gently on her shoulder. She shook it off.

❧❦❧

Tom sighed and sat beside Jamie on the warm concrete. He didn't want to lose her over this. He had to tell her. "Yes, your father hired me. I wanted to ask you if you were willing to accept me, but your father made me swear not to tell you. You wouldn't like it."

"Well, I don't." She looked up at him with a puzzled frown. "I thought I chose you. Dad asked me who I liked from my classes—someone who had the strength and intelligence to be my bodyguard, and I chose you."

"Your father advertised in the school for a bodyguard, and I was one of four on the list of applicants. Thank god, you wanted me."

"Advertised?" Her voice rose, and his hopes that she would get over this quickly fell. Jamie stood, her fists clenched. "What am I? His possession?" She wiped her eyes, as angry as he'd ever seen her.

What could he say to her? He had better get it all out now. "Maybe I did take the money because I needed it. Is that a crime? Your father picked me for good reasons. Number one, you chose me, whether you knew about the list or not. Also, I do have lots of muscular strength, because of my weight-lifting." He hesitated and spit it out. "Also, I needed the money."

"You already said that. Why? For graduate school?"

"Uh, no." He didn't want to explain, but she would keep bugging him until she got it out of him. He took a deep breath. "My father has multiple myeloma, a type of cancer they can't cure yet. It's not too serious, but he needs chemo treatments for several weeks every year. My mother died a couple of years ago, so he only has me and his brother." He wanted her to love him, not feel sorry for him, but he couldn't help accepting her arms around him. His lips crushed his smile into her cheek.

"It must have been so hard being away from him all summer, worrying. We'll be home in a couple of weeks, Tom, and you will be with him."

"Thanks for understanding," he said. "I've worried

about my father for a year now, and I was really glad your father asked me to protect you."

"Let's go finish breakfast," she said.

౿ఎౘఎ

Jamie slid in beside him in the breakfast room. After a few bites of the cold scrambled eggs, it struck her. She slammed her fork down. She pressed her eyes with the heels of her hands and straightened. "I'm still mad at Dad for hiring you. You should have told me that for sure, and you should have especially told me about your father. Now I wonder if there's anything else you're hiding. What else did Dad order you to do?"

"Take care of you, babe, because you need it. And I will." He rubbed her arm, his hand warm and gentle. "I promise."

Her anger faded a bit. He'd had a good reason not to tell her. "You did keep your word to my dad. That's good." After a long moment, she admitted, "My pride is pricked, but I guess I can still count on you." Her voice lowered. "I'm sorry, Tom." His brown eyes crinkled in his tanned face and his smile came back. She ruffled his light brown hair. "You look brown all over this morning with your tan and your brown shorts and tee."

He chuckled. "I do? You look ravishing. Your hair's still wet from the shower." He leaned close and ran his hand through her black waves. His hand on the back of her head pulled her closer. He was going to kiss her in front of everybody.

She jerked back and spoke in a low monotone. "Not now. Let's eat."

He leaned back, giving her space. "Okay, Jamie."

Gerta, the owner, approached with a coffee pot. She swirled the pot, offering the brown warmth. "You want some?"

Tom pointed to his cup. "Your place is really nice. This is a darn good breakfast for a twelve-dollar hostel: eggs, toast, an orange, and coffee. We'll be back tonight. Today we're going to explore Granada and look at the old statues in the museum."

"It's a nice city. You will enjoy the beaches by the lake. I will save a bed for you in the dormitory," Gerta replied in her thick accent.

Jamie was about to ask her if her accent was Dutch or German when her phone rang, making her jump. This hostel must have Wi-Fi. Her phone had one of those new international sim cards. It would have to be someone from home in Virginia, or her dad and stepmom honeymooning in Europe. "Hello? Who is this, please?"

"This is your Uncle James. This is Jamie Patrick, isn't it?"

"Oh yes, Uncle James, but I can't believe you're calling. Are you still in the Amazon jungle? Are you all right? Why are you calling me?"

"I'm so glad I got you, Jamie. I tried to call your father, but he's got his phone turned off while he's on his honeymoon. The maid at your house in Virginia gave me your number. Thank god for this satellite phone. I need help—soon."

"Help? What kind of help? I hope it isn't serious. Are you sick?"

"No, it's worse than that."

Jamie jerked back and turned on the speaker so Tom could hear.

"The Walaka tribe I'm staying with has been kind to me, teaching me all they know about their medicinal plants. I've been reporting quarterly what I've learned to the Indian Mission center in Ecuador, but now my tribe tells me I have to leave. I'm not sure if you know, but the local tribes have a reputation for violence. Still, despite all the warnings people gave me before I came here, I trust the tribal wise man."

"Why did they tell you to leave?"

Jamie glanced at Tom. He bent close to the phone, listening intently. Her arm went around him.

"The wise man, Chimbi, told me the neighboring Sumolu tribe doesn't like the Walaka tribe having an outsider living with them. They think all outsiders want them dead. They have seen other tribes disappear when foreigners change how they live. The Sumolus are coming to kill me after the camu camu harvest. I don't want to go, but the wise man says if I don't leave the Sumolus will come and kill all one hundred fifty of the Walaka, as well as me."

Her eyes met Tom's. "Kill you?" Her voice rose. "Good God, Uncle James, get out of there fast. You can only do so much."

"That's the problem. I called the mission in Quito. When I arrived here, the mission people 'coptered me over the Andes mountains to a town in the Amazon valley. Then I went by boat to the town nearest the Indians, Machazo. Then I walked about twenty miles into the Walaka territory. Well, the mission chief says they have a helicopter landing site at Machazo now, but their helicopter has a broken rotor, and can't be fixed in time to get me out."

Jamie grabbed Tom's arm. "Oh my God, what can we do?"

"I need you to fetch me out of here in less than two weeks."

Jamie pushed herself up from the table. Her throat tightened. "Me? I'm just a college student on vacation in Nicaragua."

The three backpacking young men in the corner had their eyes on her again.

"I'll tell you what you have to do. Fly to Quito in Ecuador. Hire a helicopter and fly to the village Machazo on the other side of the Andes mountains. I will hike the twenty miles to the village and arrive twelve days from now. That's Wednesday, September third. The mission doesn't have enough money to hire a helicopter, and I don't either. Your father pays for my work here in the jungle." His voice broke. "I depended on the mission and the helicopter. Anyway, the name of the company that rents them is Journeys into the Wilderness in Quito. Can you rent one and get me out of here?"

"Uh. Sure." Her eyes swiveled back to Tom, and he nodded yes. "What's the telephone number for the helicopter company?"

"I don't know. Here's the number for the Indian Mission. Call them and they'll help you."

She took her notebook and pen from her pack and wrote down the number as he recited it.

"You're sure you can do this?" he asked.

The tightness in her chest sparked a quick reply. *Uncle James needs me.* "Of course. We'll get you out before the Sumolu Indians come after you. I'll call you as soon as we talk to the helicopter company."

"Okay. I have to count on you. I can't see any other way. Chimbi, the wise man, is getting desperate, even angry. He'll be glad to see me leave."

"Leave earlier if you can. We will come as soon as possible, maybe even before the third. What's the name of the village again?"

"Machazo. Listen, I can't talk much longer. My satellite phone needs charging and we have no electricity here. The nearest generator is in Machazo. Call me on Monday at six o'clock. I'll keep the phone on for a half hour. You have my number on your cell, don't you?"

"Yes."

"Hope to see you a week from Wednesday. Love you, 'bye."

Jamie flopped into her chair again, a little scared.

One of the boys in the corner humphed. "You're pretty brave to go into the Amazon jungle."

"Thanks." She gave him a thin smile and turned to Tom. "When my mom died when I was little, my dad took her to a hospital in California. He was gone for months. Uncle James took care of me." Her voice softened. "He gave me ice cream every day and taught me to ride my bike." She choked at the thought and tried to cover it with a cough. Tom gave her a squeeze.

Why doesn't my father trust me or my judgment? I'm so emotional today.

Tom had out his notebook. "What's the plan, darling?"

Oooh, she did love him. He was ready to jump right in and help her, even with his own worries. "It's not going to be as easy as it sounds. Let's figure out how much money we have."

Tom shushed her. "Not so loud." He leaned in and started counting. "I have fifteen hundred."

Jamie pulled her wallet from her pack. "Five hundred," she whispered. "Leave it to my dad to insist we manage our money and refuse to give us a credit card. He turned off his phone in Europe so I can't call him to ask for more money. We have enough, if we don't help Uncle James." The seriousness of the situation sank in and her voice wavered. "If we don't help him, the Indians might kill him."

Tom gave her a tight squeeze. "What do we need?"

Jamie's fingers flew over the calculator on her phone, checking the cost of tickets.

"About a thousand to get us to Quito from the airport in Managua. Another thousand, probably, for the helicopter. Then about fifteen hundred to get us all home to Virginia." She groaned at the same time Tom did. Unthinking, she raised her voice. "Another two thousand!" She clapped her hand over her mouth. She wanted to cry.

"What'll we do? If we can't get my dad, maybe we could get some temporary funds from his partners in his medical practice. Huh, rich doctor, and he can't even help his brother escape from the jungle!"

"You don't know that." He paused a second. "I don't suppose you counted the money in my bag when you found the receipt this morning?

Her head whirled. She waited.

He leaned in close. "Your father anticipated that you might overspend," he said, "and gave me a thousand dollars for any emergency."

Great. Dad doesn't trust me at all. Acid tightened her throat and the words came out bitterly. "It's not enough. We still need another thousand for the helicopter."

"Maybe one of his partners has an emergency number to contact your father in Europe. If that doesn't work, maybe we could fly back to Virginia, get a loan really fast, and then fly to Quito and rent the helicopter."

"I tried for a loan once before and they wouldn't give it to me unless my dad signed on it, so that's out." She grimaced with pinched lips and waved her hand in the air. She couldn't figure out how to get to her uncle. She wanted her father to take care of this.

No. I have to take care of myself. I'm an adult now. Tom will help me, but I'm the one responsible for figuring out how to help Uncle James.

One of the boys from the corner walked over to them. "Sorry to listen in on your conversation. I think I can help. I've heard other backpackers who want a little cash, saying that Espinosa's Delivery Service here in Granada hires people on the spot for deliveries they have to make."

The skinny Dutch waitress plopped down beside them, coffee pot in hand. "He's right. You don't need a loan. You need a job. The delivery service is reliable. Go see him. The man who runs it is in his office after two o'clock."

Jamie had never had a job. "Thanks. Do you think we could earn enough money to get to Ecuador and rent a helicopter within the next ten days?"

The Dutch lady shrugged. "You can only try."

The backpacker went back to his breakfast and Gerta followed him.

Tom leaned closer. "I don't see any way to earn a thousand dollars that fast, Jamie. I think we should fly back to Virginia tonight. One of your father's friends will probably give us a personal loan."

Jamie's temper rose again. "No. Then I'd be obligated to my father's partner." *I'll show my father I can do it.* "I'm responsible for this myself. I like the idea of working for some money. I want to get a job."

Tom took her hand. "Okay. We'll talk to that delivery service man this afternoon after two o'clock. We can fly home tonight if we think it won't work."

"I'll make it work." She took her bag. "I'll be waiting on the front stoop."

☙❧

Tom shook his head and looked up at Gerta. "That's

my girl. And she thinks I'm not good with money. Actually, she has a heart that's too warm. She gives money away everywhere she goes. She gave a hundred dollars to support a teen-age girl's schooling in Managua, and she gave two hundred to a school for deaf kids."

Gerta sat in Jamie's chair. "Listen. I was serious about Espinosa's Delivery Service. His office is right across the square from the cathedral, next to the bank."

He took a sip of the fresh coffee, grinned, and shrugged. "Thanks. I don't think I'll convince her to ask her father's friends for money."

"Good luck with your girl."

He slung his pack over his shoulder and joined Jamie outside.

Jamie grumbled something about him not trusting her.

He didn't want another argument, so he ignored her.

She paused, picking at a weed beside the stoop. "Sorry again. I'm upset because you think I don't know how to work, that I won't be able to do the job."

He snorted and walked toward the square. "You're the one who thinks you might not be able to do a job. You finished your anthropology degree in three years. You know how to work." She didn't answer. "I promise we'll go to the delivery service office after we visit the museum this afternoon. It will be our last chance to see the statues. Whether we get a job or not, we won't be back in Granada."

The large green central plaza had a big bank on one side with guards with machine guns at the door. He ignored them. He and Jamie entered the huge cathedral that dominated the other side. Jamie's face softened and she slid onto a bench. He leaned on the back of the pew beside her and watched the birds fly in and out of the tall narrow unglazed windows. Iron bars crossed between the high arches. The birds perched and twittered. A few old women knelt in the pews.

My father will be all right, at least for the next few weeks until we get home.

Jamie said she wanted to pray for a while.

She was so beautiful with her hands folded and her black hair flowing over her shoulders. He ran his hand down her cheek, drawing a smile. "I'll wait outside and enjoy the green grass of the square."

He sat on a bench near the octagonal band stage in the center of the plaza, wondering what the Amazonian river jungles were like. Jamie was always up for new and different adventures. He wanted to help her uncle, but he wasn't so sure he wanted this adventure. Too many unknowns in a jungle. He would protect her, keep her from taking too many risks.

When Jamie came out, they bought strawberry ice cones and a hotdog from a vendor on the square. They wandered through the vegetable market and bought a bunch of carrots. The seller washed the two that they wanted and took the rest back. They munched on them while watching a man repair shoes and a dentist, with his dental chair right on the sidewalk, pulling a tooth from a wriggling customer.

She's not looking at me. Her mind is too full of how

to rescue Uncle James to see me or the poor guy in the dental chair.

The museum was actually a home for some Catholic brothers and some nuns who took care of them. Tom paid the small fee and they passed through the back wall of the gift shop to a large central courtyard.

A dozen tall palms arched their umbrellas under an incredibly blue sky, surrounded by perfect white walls of rooms roofed with red tiles, and connected with wandering white sidewalks. He loved the peaceful postcard picture and ambled slowly, enjoying the calm before the storm that would come as soon as they decided what to do to save Jamie's uncle.

Jamie looked around for the hall with the statues and pulled his tee shirt. "Over there."

About twenty statues from four to six feet high lined a gallery open to the elements on the west side.

Tom followed Jamie down the length of the gallery, studying the statues.

"Three thousand years old," she muttered. "They look like they were all done by the same stone carver. They all seem to be squatting and frowning, with those fantastic hats, crowns, on their heads."

Every chief had an animal for his crown—turtle, fox, alligator, hawk. The animals enthralled him immediately. *Why did these men choose the animals lying on their heads? For their power? What kind of power did a turtle on your head give you?*

Jamie stooped down to run her hand over a statue's hand. "The chiefs are all holding a sheaf of maize. That means they were food providers, or maybe the maize was the gift of the gods. They're different from the Mayan statues. More static, stronger. Older."

He stopped in front of a frowning chief with a jaguar on his head. The soft stone had weathered, cutting the ferocity of the animal and the chief. A stab of anxiety went through him, as if the chief were challenging him. What human instinct made him judge, even fear, the violent power of the jaguar this chief had once claimed? *Because I still have those violent instincts in me. Well, at least I'm civilized enough to control them.*

He shook off his reaction to the animal-man statues and found a shaded bench where he could sit and make notes. He wanted to remember this, even if he never took another anthropology class. Jamie seemed restless. She hurried him back out through the gift shop.

He was not as anxious as Jamie to get to Espinosa's office, but he had promised.

They walked past the bank with the machine guns in front. Tom felt the men's eyes on them, the foreigners. *They have to make sure we behave. I don't like it. I don't like guns. Jamie should know.* "Did I ever tell you about why I don't like guns?"

She looked surprised. "I didn't know you had any feelings about them at all. What happened?"

He pointed to the six inch scar on his calf below his shorts. "It was accidental, but I was angry. It kept me from being in track in high school. That's why I took up weights." He frowned and admitted, "I never forgave my friend."

"That's awful, Tom. Not the scar. Unable to forgive your friend is awful." She looked into the window of Espinosa's office. "Why are we talking about this now?"

"I just thought you ought to know." He was a bit embarrassed. He was a little afraid to tell her that he'd been so angry that he wanted to kill his friend. Why had he brought it up now? Probably because of the adrenaline thrill the Indian statue had inspired. *I'm civilized. I don't need a jaguar crown to keep Jamie and me safe.*

He opened the door for her.

Espinosa's air-conditioned office relaxed Tom. The man himself was sitting behind a desk surrounded by cabinets and a safe. No computer in sight, but a cell phone lay prominent on the desk. A short, swarthy, mustached man, he seemed the iconic Nicaraguan, even with the glasses he wore. He put down his newspaper and asked in heavily accented English if he could help them.

Jamie cleared her throat. "I certainly hope so. We need a job. Do you have work we can do?"

The man laughed, showing a lot of white teeth. "You backpackers. You are not, uhh…" He struggled for the word. "*Fidedigno.* I no trust. If I give the job to you, you want the money before the work, and you will take the money and run."

Taken aback, Tom thought about how to answer the man's implications.

Jamie's vehement reply made him smile. "We're not like that."

"Maybe. *No se.* I don't know."

Tom stepped in front of Jamie. "Sit," he told her,

pointing to a chair. She glared at him, but sat in the chair. He stepped up to the desk and put out his hand. "My name is Thomas Lee Kirk. Look, Señor Espinosa, we want a job or jobs that will provide us with two thousand dollars, not córdobas, in the next week. If that is not a possibility, just tell us right now, and we will leave." He glanced at Jamie who sat on the edge of her chair, staring at him.

Espinosa jumped up, as if he might order them out. He snapped his mouth shut and walked around them, ending at Tom's side, evaluating him. Tom pulled his hand back.

"Stop looking at me like a horse you wish to buy. Do you have a job or not?"

"Maybe." Espinosa sat down again. "You need the job bad?"

"Yes. Look, Espinosa, if you have a job like that you must need us more than we need you. We both want to earn what we need. This lady is too proud to ask her family for help. She is very hard-working." He searched his mind for the Spanish. "*Trabajador*. Admirable, don't you think?"

Espinosa blinked. "You are a señorita, but you want to work?"

"Yes," she snapped. "I am strong. I can carry things, move boxes, whatever you want me to do. I was on the rowing team for two years."

Espinosa pinched his nose and moved his glasses up on his forehead. "Okay. I guess you want the work." He pulled the glasses down and turned. "And you? Why you are here?"

Tom stood taller. "I'm stronger than she is. I worked in the coal mines with my father for two years before I entered the university. Her father hired me to protect her on this backpacking trip."

Espinosa frowned and then sat forward, his toothy smile looking false. "This is fairy tale."

Jamie picked up her backpack. "I can prove it." She took her cell phone and passport from the inside pocket and put them on the desk. "My name is Jamie Ann Patrick, which you can see on the passport. My father is a doctor. If you look at the quick dial list on my cell phone, you'll see that number two is labeled 'Office.' If you call that number they will answer, 'Gerald Patrick's Medical Practice.'"

Tom grinned. *She is smart!*

"I be damned." Espinosa picked up the phone and punched in number two. "I be damned," he repeated. Tom almost laughed. Espinosa shrugged. "Does not mean you can work."

"Give us a chance to prove it," Tom put in.

"You sit." Espinosa pointed to a second chair. He steepled his fingers.

Tom sat. *I think we're in.*

"I have the good job for two persons. You leave Managua *mañana*. You deliver heavy boxes to San Juan del Norte. You know where is San Juan del Norte?"

"No."

"We tell you how to take the boxes to the town. Important thing, this job you need to run power boat. Can you?" he asked Tom.

He opened his mouth to answer, but Jamie beat him to it. Her eyes focused on Espinosa. "Does piloting my father's race boat count? I never really raced it, but I piloted it on a three day trip on the intercoastal waterway in Florida."

Tom laughed aloud when Espinosa repeated, "I be damned."

Jamie looked utterly satisfied. "So, Señor Espinosa, how long will it take to deliver these boxes, and where is San Juan del Norte?"

The man frowned. "On Atlantic coast of Nicaragua. You will take six days if you make connections. Maybe more. Maybe nine days. You will get much money for the time—thousand dollars—each. *Bueno,* eh?"

Tom passed beyond the man's difficulty with English. Espinosa knew what they needed. *There must be a catch with that much money for a simple delivery. I'm scared. No I'm not. Jamie might think I'm a coward if I don't agree to this job. I can do this.*

Jamie opened her mouth to bargain. Tom put his hand on hers to stop her. In this part of the world, what she wanted didn't count. "Plus expenses?"

Espinosa humphed. "Yes. Deal?"

"One more question." Tom wasn't sure what answer he'd get. "Señor Espinosa, that's a lot of money to pay for six days of work. It must be very valuable product in the crates."

"Very smart, Señor Kirk. The cargo is valuable."

"Will I have to carry a gun?"

The delivery man rubbed his mustache a moment, dropped his hand to his knee to stop his foot from tapping. "No. Guns make people curious. No person can know the cargo in the boxes. We no want persons to know." Espinosa's face hardened. "You understand?"

Tom's stomach lurched. It sounded like a threat. He was ready to walk out the door.

Jamie was on her feet, though, leaning over the desk to shake Espinosa's hand. "What do we do, and where do we go?"

The stony face cracked and smiled at Jamie. He gave her hand a small shake and turned to Tom. "Take four-thirty bus to Managua. Go to the center of Managua, and take the taxi to the address I give you." He scratched the address on a piece of paper and handed it to Tom. "Managua no has street numbers or signs. Tell the taxi driver to go to the place before nine o'clock."

The paper said, *Cortez Street two blocks north of Rivera, third building on left. Guards in front of iron gate.*

Tom licked his lips.

The capital city of Nicaragua had no mailing addresses? It really was a third world country. For no apparent reason, his stomach tightened further.

"You see Roberto Estrella," Espinosa continued. "He will give you the boxes, the directions and some money for the trip. You bring the signed papers back to him, and then you get the pay money. Clear?"

"As a bell." With a big grin on her face, Jamie shook his hand again, thanking him profusely.

Tom swallowed hard and offered his hand too.

Chapter 2

Delivering for Money

As soon as she came out the door, Tom took her arm and marched her toward the bench in the plaza nearest to the bus stop.

Jamie jerked free. "My father didn't hire you to handle me. He just didn't want me to get hurt or spend my cash without thinking."

"I know that. So think about what you're doing. This job will pay you a lot of money for a short period of work, and you're willing to do it, even though this is a third-world country that runs drugs. You have no way of knowing what will be in those boxes. You heard him say it's 'valuable.' How can you take this risk? I know you want to get your uncle out of the jungle, but you are too anxious to prove that you don't need your father's help. You're only thinking of yourself."

Jamie slowed. She wanted to punch him. Why did he

always have to be right? A burst of shame filled her. She ought to think about Uncle James. When she was little, he had always let her do what she wanted, hang the consequences. Now he needed her. Her father always told her what to do, but she wasn't a spoiled brat anymore, rebelling like a teen-ager. She could do what she wanted. She didn't need her father to save Uncle James.

Thank god for Tom's common sense. *He keeps me on course.* She dragged even farther behind.

"C'mon, Jamie," Tom called from the bench. "I know what to do."

She sat beside him. "You're right. I was only thinking of myself—"

He talked over her. "First, we'll try your father's business partners. If that doesn't work we'll call *my* dad. I know he has some savings and we can pay him back later. But before we do anything we have to call the helicopter company so we know exactly how much money we need. We can call from the internet cafe."

"Okay." She picked through her bag for the telephone number for the Indian Mission. "Here. Your Spanish is better than mine."

"I'll call Journeys into the Wilderness, tell them we need the 'copter for a week, ten days from now on the thirty-first. Don't worry. I'll let them know how urgent it is."

They went to the café, and Tom phoned. He explained about Uncle James and the Indian mission's broken helicopter.

He listened for a minute. His face paled, and he sat in

the nearest chair. "Does it really have to be a whole week?" he asked her.

She nodded.

"Please reserve the helicopter from Saturday to Friday, August twenty-ninth to September fourth. We'll send two thousand dollars by Western Union immediately." He hung up. In a small voice he told her, "Two thousand dollars."

Jamie groaned. It was two thousand more than they had. She grabbed the phone and punched in her dad's office. No answer. "It's after five eastern time. This is Friday. I won't be able to get anybody until Monday." She studied her sandals. Tom's father was a retired coal miner. How could he have any savings after helping his son through college? She steeled herself. "Okay. Don't call your dad. He needs all the reserve he might have."

Tom kissed her on the top of her head. He shrugged then frowned. "We'll have to do this delivery to get the rest."

"We can do it, Tom, and I'll feel like I've done my share."

She couldn't stand sitting anymore. She jumped up, walked a few feet, circled back, and vented to Tom. "I don't know whether to be mad at my father or mad at myself. He always told me I should save for the future. I thought that meant after I had a job. He has an account for me with fifty thousand in it, but I can't have it until I'm twenty-one. I'm only twenty. My father isn't here. Dammit! I have to handle this myself."

Tom laughed. "Well, don't look at me. You always want to take care of yourself."

She kicked him lightly in the shin and left the cafe to stand in line for the four-thirty bus.

He hobbled after her crying, "Ouch, ouch. How can I work like this?"

Silly man. He made her laugh. She *would* take care of herself.

❧❧

On the crowded bus to Managua, Tom mulled over how he was losing control of the situation. How was he supposed to keep them both safe? He didn't want Jamie to think he was afraid, but she was so worried about her uncle that she wasn't thinking sensibly about the risks.

Jamie asked him details about how he got his scar. Then her fingers rubbed the scar and sent shivers up his leg until he began to get stiff. Good thing these shorts were loose.

He really wanted to make love to this blue-eyed raven-haired beauty. With her pale skin, she was what his father called "Black Irish." He itched to give her what she wanted, but she kept resisting.

We spent the whole summer sleeping in separate beds. It's time to get a fancy hotel room and start exploring each other. She had looked so great this morning coming out of the community shower wrapped in a towel, with her wet hair shining. When he had reached for the towel, she had slapped his hand away.

I know she wants it. Whenever I hug her she curls

right up to me. She smells so good. Those pheromones are working, both hers and mine.

As they approached Managua, they moved to the front of the bus.

"Hey, Jamie, let's get off at this mall and have dinner before we commit ourselves to possible illegal smuggling."

"Good idea."

Jamie loved the mall. "This seems like New York. The air-conditioning feels so good. Look. A café with hamburgers and salads. My kind of place."

They didn't talk once about THE JOB. It was close to eight and quite dark by the time they left.

"I'm going to ask Estrella straight out if we will be smuggling drugs," he told Jamie in the taxi. "I don't want to do this if it's illegal. For both our sakes."

Jamie hesitated, her tone becoming serious. "I've decided to do what's necessary to save Uncle James, and also to show my father I'm not relying on him anymore, but I know you're right. We could ruin our entire lives if we got involved in drug smuggling." She leaned over and kissed him on the cheek. "Thank you for doing the thinking about this."

Whew, he thought, maybe she really is growing up. His cheek was still warm where she kissed him. Maybe tonight.

Managua didn't have street lights either. When they circled around a block, the taxi driver explained that he had to be careful in this neighborhood because sometimes people stole manhole covers to sell the metal for money.

They pulled up in front of a ten foot high wall with a large barred gate leading into a paved courtyard. Two guards stood outside the gate with machine guns. Tom swallowed his tension while Jamie argued with the taxi driver, who wanted to charge five hundred córdobas. She gave him half.

Tom handed the guard on the right the note from Espinosa with the address on it. "We're here to see Roberto Estrella before nine o'clock."

The other guard walked in front of the gate with his Kalashnikov trained on Tom, not Jamie.

Tom explained in his schoolbook Spanish. "I'm here to do a job for Sr. Estrella. Sr. Espinosa from Granada sent me." He knew better than to mention Jamie.

However, she couldn't keep her mouth shut. In her more colloquial Spanish, she told the guard to hop to it, or he would be in trouble with his boss if she had to telephone Espinosa. She threw in a couple of swear words.

The husky guard with the cleft chin stepped forward, pointing his machine gun at her now. "Who is this woman? Women don't do deliveries for Sr. Estrella."

"She takes care of the paperwork." Tom took out his phone. "Do I have to call Sr. Espinosa?"

Cleft chin ordered them to wait. He unlocked the gate and disappeared into the courtyard for a long five minutes. When he returned, he handed Tom a flashlight and gestured them in.

"Up those stairs. Sr. Estrella is in the office at the end of the hall."

Tom hooked his arm through Jamie's, and they

walked through the moonlit courtyard past two Ford commercial vans. After he flashed the light into the open doorway Jamie took the light and lit the way up the narrow metal stairway. Their shoes clanked on the steps.

Jamie whispered hoarsely, "Don't touch the wall. It's filthy." They stepped through the open door at the top. The hallway was a metal-railed balcony. "Looks like a factory."

"Yeah, but what kind of factory?"

It was too dark to get any clue of the first floor in the airless depths. Electric light beamed from the open door of the office at the end of the hall.

Roberto Estrella was fat and old. His remaining hair was short and his nose bulbous, but the voice that boomed from the body was loud and friendly. Overenthusiastic, Tom thought. He wore a sport coat several sizes too small and a short tie.

"Sit down, you two youngsters." His English was better than Espinosa's. He gestured to the two chairs in front of his desk. The light was a single bulb hanging from the ceiling and the air-conditioning was a single fan. Papers littered his desk, but the ubiquitous cell phone lay in the empty space in the center. "Let us talk. I'm Roberto Estrella and you are?"

"I'm Tom Kirk and this is Jamie Patrick. Espinosa's Delivery Service said you have a job for us. Didn't he call you?"

"He wasn't sure you would show up."

Tom cleared his throat. This was the time to say it. *He won't kill us for asking.* "Señor Estrella, Espinosa told us you would pay us two thousand dollars for a week's work delivering some crates for you. That is an inordinate amount of money for this work, especially in this country. We are Americans and we want to be certain this doesn't involve smuggling drugs."

Estrella shook his large corpus no. "Drugs?" He threw his head back and gave a hearty laugh, which didn't strike Tom as sincere. "Oh no, I don't smuggle drugs. I would never do that. It's illegal. They might catch me and then I'd have to bribe a bunch of government officials to stay out of jail. They would make a lot of money, but I wouldn't." He laughed again, shaking his head. "No, I wouldn't do that. You can count on it."

Jamie heaved a sigh of relief at his side.

She's too trusting, Tom thought. He wondered what the man was hiding. "What is it that we will be transporting?"

Another loud laugh. "If you insist, I will tell you, but you must not tell anyone else. It will be dangerous for you if anyone else knows. The crates are full of diamond core samples from a drilling rig. They are cylinders of stone grit with raw diamonds in them, from a mine in South America. I won't tell you where. I wouldn't want you to be tempted to sell the information to anyone else." He looked sharply at Tom, suddenly seeming more intelligent. "But you wouldn't do that, would you? Two college graduates like you?"

Jamie piped up. "We're pretty desperate for money, but not for ourselves. It's to save someone's life. You can rely on us."

Estrella jerked his head to examine Jamie. Apparently he hadn't expected her to have anything to say.

Uneasy at her unthinking boldness, Tom leaned on the desk. "With two of us doing this important delivery for you, we should probably ask for twice the money. After all, no one is likely to expect a young couple in love of transporting anything important."

He had a hard time not laughing when Jamie swung around open-mouthed.

Estrella frowned. "We'll see about that when you complete the delivery successfully."

Tom nodded and caught Jamie's eye. Estrella really needed them. Tom was glad he had dared to ask for more. "Tell us the details of what we have to do."

"I am sending the cores to the mining company's headquarters in New York. They will go by boat from San Juan del Norte, a small port on the Atlantic coast. Your job is to get them to the port. If you agree to do the job, you will both write the directions on a piece of paper and then sign your names. I will copy the agreements before you leave."

Tom nodded and got out his notebook. Jamie did too.

"First, the crates are already loaded in one of the vans outside. You will drive it to Granada for the night, get up early tomorrow, and go to the ferry station on Lake Nicaragua. Don't worry about directions. I will give you a map. Load the crates on the ferry trip across the lake that leaves at eleven o'clock. Don't forget to buy tickets for yourselves. It will take four hours on the ferry to get to Ometepe, the island in the middle of the lake. The ferry will dock at the island for an hour. Be on it when it leaves. It will take another six hours to get to San Carlos on the southern end of Lake Nicaragua. Unload the crates and hire a boat. Load them on the boat and go down the San Juan River to the ocean. It will take two days. Stop at El Castillo overnight. Do not take time to sight see. Deliver the crates to Guillermo Montoya in San Juan del Norte. He has a warehouse next to the docks. He will take care of transporting them from that point. He has, uh, boats. Then you can reverse the trip and come here to receive your pay. Bring back the paperwork with his signature. Any questions?"

They had both written as fast as they could, to keep up. It wasn't like taking notes in a class. Tom compared his to Jamie's to make sure neither of them had missed any detail.

"I want you to add one more clause to this contract. One of you shall always be with the crates, twenty-four hours a day, even at night. Tonight, tomorrow, and every hour of this trip until you turn them over to Montoya. Write it down, sign the contract and give it to me. I'll make copies and then join you downstairs with the expense money."

Tom signed. This would not be easy. A lot of work loading and unloading. Not being able to sleep even in the same room with Jamie. He hoped the van would be comfortable.

Jamie tapped her teeth with the pen. She signed the contract and gave it to Estrella. Tom followed her out of the claustrophobic office down the railed walkway to the stairs. She stopped and flashed the light over the railing again to see what was on the first floor. Only stacks of crates as far as Tom could see.

Their feet clanked again on the metal stairs. When they walked over to the vans the heavy-set guard with his gun came to watch them. The back doors of one of the vans hung open. Tom lifted the black canvas covering the contents. Two large crates, about a meter wide, a half-meter deep and two meters long sat under eight more boxes a meter wide and a half-meter deep, but only a meter long. In addition, ten boxes about a foot square lay on top. None of the containers had labels. Tom reached over to move one of the boxes and the guard waved him away with his gun.

Tom jumped back. "I only wanted to see how much they weigh."

Stacked on their sides, they filled the bed of the van a meter and a half high.

Estrella came downstairs huffing and handed the córdobas to Tom to put in his bag, but he didn't have room. Estrella went back up and brought down a gym bag to put the money in.

"How much are you giving us for expenses?" Jamie asked.

"Forty thousand córdobas. That's about fifteen hundred dollars. It should be enough to rent the boat for five days and more than enough for food and hostels. Remember, don't have a conversation with anybody and tell them what you're carrying."

"We'll follow your orders. We'll earn this money."

"Yes, I'm certain you will. Leave now for Granada. You should arrive by midnight. One of you will get a good night's sleep. Good luck."

Why do we need good luck? The real dangers of this trip began to press into Tom.

Chapter 3

Across Lake Nicaragua

The next morning Jamie came out of Gerta's hostel and peeked in the front window of the van. Empty.

"Yoo-hoo, where are you?" She opened the back doors. The two stretch cords holding the canvas over the crates were unhooked and the lump on top of the crates wrapped in the canvas must be Tom. She thumped on the boxes with her fist. "Wake up. Do you want breakfast? Gerta's waiting."

She kissed him lightly after he climbed down, moaning and groaning. "The boxes are hard, and the air was stifling with the doors closed, but at least I could stretch out."

"Go get your breakfast. I'll watch the—" She stopped before "diamonds" came out. "—boxes. It's almost seven and we have to get to the ferry boat landing.

Maybe Gerta has a blanket and pillow we can take with us."

She pushed her hair, still wet from the shower, behind her ears. Her eyes surveyed Tom, the bodyguard with the sleepy eyes and the muscular arms under the tight green tee shirt. A morning desire moved her closer, and she reached up to move her fingertips along his cheek. He closed to her, blocking the sun behind him. She could see every whisker and a small scar on his chin. He was a man and she wanted him. She couldn't help it.

She dropped her pack, and, after a moment's hesitation, he wrapped his arms around her, holding her close along the whole length of her body. She couldn't turn away from the good warmth inside, and her arms hugged him back without reserve.

His soft lips on her cheek lowered to kiss her neck under her ear and then slid over her cheek. They reached her mouth and seared her lips. She surrendered and let him do as he willed. His tongue flicked into her mouth and he pulled his hips tight to her belly. Her insides melted and she sagged into him. His lips wandered to her cheek again with little bites teasing her. Then his mouth was hard on hers. She gave him everything she dared, standing outside in the parking lot.

When she finally pushed him away, she put her hand on his solid chest and then to her hot face. "Tom, I can hardly catch my breath. So much for waiting." His grin widened when she kissed him again on the cheek and swatted his bottom. "Get going."

She sat in the truck and re-read Estrella's instructions

about ten times, as she turned her mind slowly from Tom's kiss and the new situation. *What made me change? Call it lust, passion, hormones. I guess it's silly to wait two more weeks.*

For the hundredth time, she wondered what her uncle was doing right now in the jungle. Probably making breakfast—boiled yucca roots?—before collecting plants. How many specimens would he be bringing this time? Two years ago, he had brought home a trunk full of dried specimens in plastic bags. Her father and he had talked about whether it was feasible to use the Indian tribe as a source for plants that they could turn into health food supplements. It would have to be approved by the FDA and who knows what other government lettered organizations. She was deep into the realization that she didn't know enough chemistry when Tom climbed into the van.

"I stuffed two pillows and two blankets and my pack on top of the square boxes in the back. You want me to put your pack and the gym bag in the back?"

Jamie blushed, wondering what he thought of her kiss, not daring to ask. She glanced at the pack under her feet. "Don't bother."

The first sight of Lake Nicaragua turned this trip into an adventure. "Wow. Look at the whitecaps." She stuck her head out the window and gave a whoop. "This is better than old Indian statues. Gerta says it's a third the size of Lake Michigan, all fresh water. Pollution and fishermen killed off the sharks that used to live in it. I love the water."

"Sharks? I don't believe it." He pulled into the large

empty parking lot next to the ticket building to pay for the transport. It cost thirty-six hundred córdobas, about one hundred forty US dollars, to carry the boxes to San Carlos at the southern end of the lake.

Jamie was impressed. "Seven dollars a box. Not bad. I hope they have enough room for people,"

The clerk laughed. "We make more money on passengers than cargo. You will be surprised how many people we stuff around the freight. Take your truck, back it up to where the dock is, and carry your cargo on. The captain will show you where and how to stack your crates, and he'll charge you for a net to keep your cargo in place."

"Thanks," Tom said. "Oh, can we leave the van here for when we get back in a week? Here's ten bucks if you'll keep it in that fenced area back there."

"Certainly, sir."

"You really think ahead, Tom. It's not even eight o'clock. If we get to work, maybe we can get it done before anyone else arrives."

"Okay. I'll move the van."

I suppose he thinks he has to do it because he's a man. Well, I can carry heavy things. I've been carrying this pack all summer.

Tom opened the doors and they put the blankets, pillows, and packs on top of the gym bag in the front seat. In ten minutes they had the boxes stacked on the ground. Then they carried one of the big boxes down the dock and onto the ferry. It was heavy and hard to carry with no handles. She took the front and he took the back, pushing her forward at his pace. At least the gangplank had rails so that if she lurched she wouldn't fall into the water. Jamie dropped her end as soon as they reached the middle of the stern deck. It landed with a loud boom as it slipped out of her hands behind her. She screeched and Tom hollered at her. "Next time warn me when you're going to drop it."

"Sorry."

A man strolled over. He was as tall as Tom, a well-muscled man wearing a blue short-sleeved uniform shirt and a captain's hat. "I'm Captain Ricardo. How many crates do you have?"

"Another one like this, and eight more almost as big as these two, and four boxes a half-meter square. Where do we put them? Do you have a hold?"

"No. We're flat bottomed. Your heavy crates might shift if we get a rain storm and the waves get high. What's in them?"

Tom swallowed. "Uh…"

Jamie's stomach lurched. "Car parts," burst out of her. "They're opening a garage in San Juan del Norte and this is their first shipment of parts. You know, axles, drive trains, batteries. Heavy stuff like that." Both men stared at her as if she were an alien. What was their problem?

Tom shook his head. "Uh, yeah. Where should we put them?"

The captain probably thought he was a bit slow. Apparently Tom wasn't used to lying. She covered her twitching mouth and looked around while the captain explained that for balance he wanted half of them on the large deck at the stern end of the boat and the other half on the small forward deck in front. Then he specified how to stow them so they wouldn't shift. Tom would have to buy a net for the stern deck, but he could use the stretch cords and canvas from the van for the bow deck.

The rectangular ferryboat had a large cabin in the middle. Bored with the talk, Jamie wandered down the middle aisle between the two rows of ten foot long benches. Twenty benches. Maybe a hundred passengers if it was full. She wasn't looking forward to it. *I hope they have a bathroom. I mean a head. They have to have one, but I bet it just drains into the lake. The pollution killed those sharks.*

Tom called that he was ready to get the rest of the boxes. "I'm afraid to leave the van sitting without one of us in it. What if someone else gets here early to load their stuff? Maybe you should just stay by the boxes while I move them."

"How? By yourself? Besides, we can see the van from the boat. Let's move this next big one."

When they got back to the truck, Tom wanted to ask at the ticket window if he could hire a man to help move the boxes. It made Jamie angry. Why did men always assume she couldn't do what she said?

"No way. I wanted this job, and I have to help. We can carry two boxes on top of each other and cut the trips in half." *I'm still out of breath from the first two crates. Can I do it? I will.*

She tried, but the top box kept slipping because she

couldn't hold it steady. It would have to be one at a time.

"It's hard," she told Tom. "I guess I used different muscles when I was on the rowing team."

"Don't complain. It takes too much breath."

"Yeah."

After they carried the eight medium boxes forward the captain sent his mate Julio to give them a hand and make sure they secured them properly. They stacked the eight boxes on one side of the canvas from the truck, wrapped it around the crates and fixed it to the rails with the stretch cords. The square crates were as heavy as the two big crates. Tom thought they each weighed about a hundred pounds. He carried the last two small boxes himself when passengers started arriving, and she guarded their stack on the stern deck. She stood at the side so she could watch the stack on the forward deck. They finished by nine-thirty.

Tons of people were lining up for tickets. Two trucks pulled in with other people's loads. Jamie was exhausted, but she didn't say it out loud to Tom. She leaned back on the rail resting and enjoying the hustle and bustle. Lots of people had lunchboxes or bags with food for the day. Oops. They would need some.

"Tom, would you go get us some food for the day? I'll stay here to watch our stuff. You can probably find some on the road by the beach."

"Love to." He waited a moment longer. "I wish you could come with me. I know you love the water."

"Don't worry. I promise to be envious, and you'll have to kiss me again."

After he was gone, she watched the cabin fill with sweaty milling passengers. On the back deck, large cloth bags of coffee beans and nuts and plastic bags of clothes and tourist hats and sunglasses hid their crates. She couldn't even see them. Passengers sat on the deck floor around them. Nobody could reach their crates if they tried.

Tom came back with some sandwiches, a box of fried chicken and two mangoes. Yum. He didn't seem tired at all. He carried their packs and the blankets and pillows from the truck to the forward deck. With the truck safely locked behind the fence, he brought the gym bag full of cash and sat beside her on the deck.

"It's so crowded I guess we won't have to watch the crates back here," he whispered in her ear. "What a relief. Let's go check the front deck." He walked along the narrow starboard deck outside the cabin.

"I'm going through the cabin," she called after him.

Inside, people pushed their way past other people loaded with bags and lunch boxes, looking for a seat, but every seat seemed taken or saved by bags. Small arguments about who deserved a seat erupted in two places just in the time she strolled down the aisle. One gal tried to hog a whole bench by lying down on it. That didn't last long. Two men bodily forced her to sit up. At the front of the cabin people gathered to buy bottled water and cans of soda from one of the crew. She walked past the head and out the door to Tom.

Past the stairway up to the wheel room, they found their black canvas pile undisturbed. She'd watched them from her perch at the rail on the front deck. Nevertheless, two men seemed to have walked down the port side and settled in this spot unseen.

Her heart jerked. *I have to do a better job watching the diamonds.*

Tom nodded to them. "Guess we'll join you and sit out here. It's not so crowded."

The men went back to their conversation.

Jamie folded her blanket in a tight square and set it beside her pack. She joined Tom at the rail and leaned over to see if she could see anything in the water. "Look at the oil from the engines. Pollution, ugh. They say it's overfished too."

"Haven't thought much about the pollution, but then I'm not a fisherman. Maybe I should. On the other hand, I love the air."

"Think I'll store up some energy for moving those boxes off the boat tonight when we get to San Carlos." She sat on her comfy folded blue blanket and leaned back on the stack of crates. She leaned sideways onto the pillow on top of her case and closed her eyes. She never napped during the day, but was almost out. The engines thrummed a lullaby beneath her. She smiled and felt safe for the moment with Tom beside her.

Jamie woke with a start. She jumped up to stand beside Tom, still at the rail. "What's going on?"

"Nothing. That was quite a power nap you took. An hour. Relax. We have three hours of vacation until we get to Omotepe."

"Great. I'm going to walk around for a bit."

Tom waved her off. She passed the smelly head and entered the cabin. People had settled and only normal conversation seethed around her. She bought a bottle of water. A woman brushed past her in the narrow central aisle with her little boy hurrying to the head.

"Cute, isn't he?" the older woman next to her asked. "Do you want to sit here until my daughter gets back?"

"Sure. Tell me why it's so crowded. Where are all these people going? They don't look like tourists."

The old lady chuckled. "No, we're too poor. Most of us are going to San Carlos and then on to Costa Rica by bus. We're looking for jobs. Costa Rica has more tourists than Nicaragua, so more jobs."

"What sort of work do you do?"

"I just watch my grandson. My daughter makes a living as a lady of the night. It's not the best kind of work, but we get by."

Startled by the woman's open admission, Jamie decided to move on. Besides, the daughter and her boy were coming back. "*Hasta la vista.* See you later."

The people around her didn't seem desperate. Whatever the reason, their moral standards had slipped. Her conscience slapped her. *What vanity. Don't think you're better than other people. Didn't you decide this morning that you couldn't wait any longer for Tom?*

Out on the crowded back deck men sat in groups in front of the freight pile or leaned on the rail. Three men squatted around a pile of córdobas playing cards. A blonde girl and her boyfriend were speaking English to an Italian-looking guy.

Jamie sidled up to them and asked if they were back-packers too.

"Yes, we are going to the island to hike up the volcano. Are you going also?"

"No, we're going on to San Carlos."

She stayed and talked for a while, enjoying the receding coast, watching the flocks of white birds flying back and forth. The Swedish girl asked if she had seen the horses running along the beach this morning. Apparently some men with horses who did work in Granada lived close to the beach, and ran their half-dozen horses up the sandy strand past the fenced and gated houses until they got to the open area just before the ferryboat parking lot.

"That area, you know, where the homeless live," the Swede went on. "We walked over and talked to some of them this morning. Did you see them? They build shacks out of pieces of wood and boxes with plastic tarps over them. Then they steal water and electricity from the city government. They have nothing at all."

"It sounds gruesome. People will do anything to stay alive. Nicaragua has a lot of desperate people," Jamie concluded. After talking about Swedish government and Italian food for a while, Jamie's hunger started to make demands. "I'm going back to my boyfriend on the forward deck and eat my lunch now. Would you like to join us? It's not so crowded."

They bought bottles of water in the cabin and settled on the front deck to enjoy lunch. It was all very pleasant until the girl started asking questions about them. "Are you going to get married? Why are you backpacking in Central America? Why are you going to San Carlos? Why don't you stop at Omotepe Island with us? You could climb the volcano with us. This is your stuff? Oh, you're just delivering it? What is it? It must be really valuable if you have to guard it."

Jamie could see Tom was getting nervous. He stood. "That's enough questions," he said gruffly. "Jamie needs to rest. She's pregnant. I'll walk with you to the back deck and let her nap, okay?"

Jamie's head rose at that, but nobody noticed.

They agreed and left Jamie alone.

She leaned against the "car parts." *Tom is learning to lie. He probably doesn't like it, but it seems necessary to protect these damn diamond cores. Why aren't they all the same size? Estrella could have lied to us. I'll talk to Tom about it later. My goodness, so I'm pregnant. Maybe someday it will be true.* She rose and leaned against the rail, thinking about it. *I'm glad I told Tom I'm not a virgin. I don't want him to hold back.*

Tom left her alone for quite a while. They could see one of the two volcanoes on the island in the distance when he came back. "I had a nice talk with the captain. Since we are anthropologists, he thinks we would like to see the old Indian statues in the church graveyard. It seems they are very similar to the ones in the Granada museum. It's only a five minute walk to the church, and if we want to go together, he'll watch our car parts. I don't know if we should take a chance like that, but I would like to see the statues. The ones in the museum had a powerful effect on me."

"I'm not as interested as you, and I can watch the crates on the back deck. You go right away and maybe I can go see them afterward. I'd love to climb the volcano someday, but it's miles away on the south side of the island." She half-smiled at him. "Besides I'd better stay here and rest because I'm pregnant. Does the captain know?"

"No. Let me make it true when we get to San Carlos."

With lots of clangs and bangs and bumps the large ferry docked at the ten foot pier, and the sailors put a narrow gang-plank down to a white gravel open area the size of a football field.

Tom kissed her and left. Uneasy about letting him go, she worried whether he would fall off the narrow plank with only a chain for a rail. She worried he wouldn't get back in time. *Oh, he will. He's so reliable. I can count on him.*

She clamped down on her mind and went back to the front deck to observe. She was careful to stand where she could see the crates on the stern deck too. Only ten people debarked, most carrying large sacks of whatever they had bought on the mainland.

Then the captain and his small crew helped two others to unload sacks of packaged goods for the island. He spoke to the man who had helped them secure the boxes this morning and pointed to her.

The sailor approached her. "Captain Ricardo wants to talk to you," he said and left.

The captain took her arm and led her around the corner of the cabin. She couldn't see their crates on the deck at the bow. At the stern, trade goods still covered their boxes. Two new passengers added sacks of fragrant oranges and bananas from the island to sell in San Carlos.

"Miss Patrick, do you know the man whose boxes you are accompanying to San Juan del Norte?"

A sharp breath of anxiety filled her. "No. An independent delivery service hired us to take these car parts to the new garage. It's not really any of your business, is it?" She hoped he didn't hear the trembling in her voice.

"Not usually, but last month we carried boxes of similar shapes and sizes to San Juan del Norte. Two young backpackers guarded that shipment. I don't suppose they are opening two garages in that town."

Oh dear. This is bad. Where's Tom? "You deliberately sent Tom to look at those statues!" she accused.

The captain nodded. "I wanted you to go also, but you decided to be careful. That's good."

You think so? "What do you want?"

"My man Julio is opening one of the boxes on the front deck right now. We want to be certain it isn't drugs or guns."

Oh my god. She ran along the cabin toward the back. *If he steals the diamonds, how will I get Uncle James back?*

"I won't be involved in anything illegal," the captain called, trailing after.

Julio had unhooked the canvas and was prying the lid off a box.

"Stop! Don't open it. It's not yours."

The crowbar thunked on the deck and he raised his hands and backed away. "It's too late. I already broke the seal. We caught you now."

"Caught us?" Jamie screeched, grabbed the crowbar from the deck, and ran at him, ready to whack him. "My uncle will die if you don't leave these crates alone."

He laughed, caught her arm, and she struggled for a minute before she gave up and backed away. It was useless. He was too burly and strong.

"Just a little bitch from America smuggling drugs."

"I am not! You don't have the right to look at our stuff," she hollered, getting in his face.

The captain pulled her away, but she shook him off too. He waved Julio back to work. "Go supervise the rest of the loading." He let go of her elbow. "Now tell me what's in your heavy crates, or I will call the police when we get to San Carlos."

"The police?" She turned away from the captain, wanting to cry. What would her father think? What would become of Uncle James? "You can't call the police. My uncle will die."

"Why? Maybe I'm saving him from a life of crime or an early death from overdose."

Insulted, she burst out the explanation. "My uncle is a medical doctor and a botanist. He studies plants in the Amazon River basin. He saves lives, and we need the money we get for delivering these boxes to hire a helicopter to pick him up before he's killed by a bunch of headhunters." *He'll never believe that.*

The captain sighed. "Do you know what's in the crates? I'm being patient with you."

Should she admit that she wasn't sure? Captain Ricardo looked toward the gangplank. Tom was back.

Oh my god!

Tom was struggling with Julio. Tom pushed him away, but Julio grabbed his tee, swung him around and pounded his face. Tom's arm came up and punched the man in the temple. Julio backed away, his hand to his head.

"Where is she?" Tom hollered.

Passengers exchanged worried looks and one started toward Tom.

"Here I am," she called.

Tom ran to her down the narrow walkway beside the cabin and wrapped his arms around her.

He wiped the tears from her face with his hand. "Stop crying. It's all right. I'm here." He scowled at the captain. "That guy told me I had to stay away from the forward deck. What did they do to you?"

"Don't look at me," Ricardo said. "She tried to hit Julio with a crowbar. You two stay right here for the next half hour. I have to run this ferry. As soon as we leave the island, I want to see what's in those crates. If it's anything illegal, I'm turning you over to the police in San Carlos. Do you understand?"

Tom nodded and the captain went up the stairs to the wheelhouse.

She was mad again for a second. The captain didn't tell Tom her side of the story. Well, at least they would get a look at the diamond cores. She gently ran her hand over Tom's red bruised face.

Chapter 4

Delivering Diamonds

Jamie's hand calmed Tom, and the shaking inside eased. He had actually hit that man, and the captain was threatening the police. What a mess.

"When I came back to the ferry, that jerk Julio tried to keep me from coming to this deck. I probably have a black eye now. Haven't had one since I was a kid. I bet Julio has one. How about you? Why are you crying? Tell me what happened." He sat her on her folded blanket and squatted next to her, leaning on the loose canvas.

"Julio was watching our cargo because the captain wanted to talk to me. The captain lured me away so Julio could look in the boxes to see what we had. I tried to stop him. If Julio opened them, we wouldn't be able to deliver the boxes. I picked up the crowbar Julio dropped on the deck and swung it at him, but he grabbed me and made me drop it." Jamie rubbed her arm. "I know I have a tem-

 Carol J. Megge

per, but I don't think I would have hurt him. I was so worried about Uncle James and what my father might do if he came home from Europe and found us in jail in Nicaragua." She wet her lips, feeling tentative. "Do you believe me?"

He humphed. "Look what I did. Gave Julio a black eye, and I'm proud of it. We all have some of that in us." *Maybe I really am that kind of man, a little uncivilized. Now I know why the Indian chief wore the jaguar on his head three thousand years ago.*

Jamie patted his knee.

The motors hummed and the deck throbbed.

Tom stood and lifted the canvas. He pulled Jamie up. "Let's look at this open box before Captain Ricardo forces us. If it's illegal, we'll turn the load over to the authorities."

"Good idea. If it's not diamonds we'll just have to figure a way to get out of the police's hands by Monday. Then we can call my dad's partners for money to rescue my uncle."

Tom stared at the second-story wheelhouse looking down on them. "I wonder if the captain can see us. He'll be down soon. Do you know what a diamond core looks like?"

"Well, I know the diamonds won't be cut and polished. They'll just be dull stones."

"Yeah. They probably will be too small to see visibly in the core. Here goes." He pulled the lid off and leaned over the crate, hoping his back blocked the view from the wheelhouse. "Stand beside me."

Whew. Three-meter-long cylinders, maybe forty centimeters in diameter, wrapped in a heavy gray plastic, filled the crate, side by side. "Let's see how heavy they are. Take that end." They raised it a foot. "Feels like about eighty pounds. Does that sound right for a solid piece of rock?"

Jamie put her side down. "It is heavy. Mmm. I don't know if it's heavy enough. Maybe it's not solid. Maybe the core from the drilling rig is broken in pieces and stored in a steel tube."

"I didn't hear anything sliding when you put your end down."

"What do you think is in those cylinders?" The captain stood right behind him.

Tom's heart jerked. He jumped sideways. Jamie cringed.

Captain Ricardo stepped up to the crate and ran his hand over the cylinder they had moved. "It's not car parts. What is it?" His muscles rippled as he lifted it. "It is heavy."

"Jamie, get out our contracts. We'll have to show him." Tom reached out to the captain, while Jamie dug in her pack for the papers. "We have proof."

The captain brushed Tom's hand off, anger in his voice. "Don't touch me. I have no idea what kind of people you are, or what this cargo is."

"Okay." Tom noticed that the captain wore a gun belt, with a pistol on his right side. His hand was on it. "Look, Captain Ricardo, our employer assured us our cargo is legal. We're just students, and we need money to hire a helicopter to fly over the Andes Mountains to a village in the rain forest. We need to bring her uncle out of the jungle where he's been working with a primitive tribe before they kill him. We have nothing to prove that, but it's true. We do have proof of our contract for this delivery."

"Yes." Jamie shoved her contract into the captain's hands. "It says we are to deliver twenty crates to the port of San Juan del Norte within ten days."

"Show me where it says what's in the crates."

Jamie pointed out the sentences about diamond cores on the second page. It listed the twenty boxes and their sizes and weights.

Tom peered into the crate. It certainly looked like diamond cores. He could be sure if he had X-ray vision. He laughed at himself. It had been years since he had longed for super powers. Working in a coal mine had killed those illusions. Nowadays, he got what he worked for. He hoped it was enough for Jamie.

The captain shook his head. "Since I can't see into those steel cylinders, I can't tell what's in them. I don't think drugs would be that solid and heavy. Nothing is sliding around. I don't see why Estrella shipped a similar shipment last month, but I do understand why he directed you to keep silent about what you are delivering. It is possibly worth more than drugs. If another shipment comes through on this ferry next month, I will report it to the government." He patted the tubes. "I won't take you to the police. I'll assume you are telling the truth because you have a contract, despite that ridiculous story about your uncle. You have a dangerous job. Stay away from the crew and the rest of the passengers until we get to San Carlos tonight. You can debark after everyone else is gone." The captain interrupted Tom's thanks. "That is for my safety as well as yours. I don't want the San Carlos police roaming my boat looking for bribes. Don't get into any more fights." He left.

Tom avoided looking up at the wheelhouse window. Julio was probably piloting the boat.

Jamie's arm went around his. "Let's close this box before any passengers wander back here," she whispered. "I'm afraid to say anything out loud now. At least half of the people on this boat are desperate for jobs. Who knows what they might be willing to do." They shoved the loose cylinder back into its tight-fitting slot in the crate. They slid the nails protruding from the lid back into their holes in the crate and pushed down hard until the lid felt solid.

"We'll buy some nails and a hammer at the hardware before we leave in the morning and tighten it. I think we can relax for a few hours now." He moved Jamie's hair out of her mouth where she was chewing on the end. "Don't look so worried. We'll be fine." *I hope.*

"I'm not so much worried about us as I am about Uncle James. I don't want to fail him. We have to do this job, no matter how dangerous it is. I never had to worry about money before. No wonder people get desperate."

"You're braver than you thought." *Braver than me.*

Jamie pulled him close, her words in his ear quiet and penetrating. "It's not that I'm so brave. It's just that I never had to commit to anything important before. I can't *not* do this for Uncle James." She leaned on the railing, looking south, as if to the Amazon jungle.

His arms went around her from behind, closing the whole length of her body to his. He wanted to comfort and protect her. Her body was soft and warm, yet firm with determination. Did she get how much he admired her? How to say it? "Jamie, no matter what you think about your father, I love you, darling, and I'll protect and help you all the way, because you're *my* commitment." He turned her around to face him. "You know I mean that, don't you?"

She snuggled against him. "I know you'll protect me when I need it, and not because my father paid you. As for more than that, I'm sure it's coming. What more do you want? Isn't pretending I'm pregnant enough?" She giggled and didn't try to move from his grasp.

Could she feel his arousal stirring? He dampened his desire. *Later.*

Instead, he told her about the cemetery by the church on the island. "I walked past the crosses and old stone plaques to the back of the cemetery. The eight statues are so weathered the Indians' faces are indistinguishable. You can't tell what animal they had chosen for their crowns. They disturbed me more than the ones in Granada. They seem to have lost their power. Still, I felt them challenging me—the animal part of me at least, as if I might lose *my* power. I suppose that's why I reacted to Julio the way I did. Sorry you didn't get to see them."

Jamie was chewing her hair again. "I'm losing interest in these ancient Indian tribes anyway. I don't care if I don't get to see them. I am interested in the tribes in the Amazon, though. I want to know how they live, and about those plants that could replace artificial antibiotics. Their ancient knowledge fascinates me."

"I know what you mean. I'm trying to figure out what area to concentrate on in grad school next year. Maybe I'll change to these present-day South American Indians. I've heard they're still in the Stone Age, with handmade tools. No metals. I can't imagine how they survive." He shuddered. "What do they do if they get poisoned by a frog or bitten by a snake? I know they have their shamans like our North American Indians have medicine men. They make the curare for their arrows. I need to know more chemistry."

Jamie tucked her arm through his. "That's great. I didn't know you were thinking of changing your major. Me too. I can't wait to talk to my uncle. I want to learn more about the plants. I'll have to take some botany and chemistry classes too."

The hours passed. The huge reach of Lake Nicaragua's fairly smooth waters became boring to Tom, especially since they could not leave the forward deck. Look at the danger he had caused by leaving Jamie alone for fifteen minutes. He did send her to the back deck several times to sniff out if anyone was interested in their cargo. No one asked her about it.

Jamie laughed at his black eye, which was actually turning bright purple. He checked it out in the mirror in the lavatory. It was less lurid than the sunset, and not that visible now that it was dark.

They ate the rest of the chicken, wishing they had more.

As they finally approached the dock in San Carlos it was ten-thirty, too dark to see what the city was like, not that they would have any time to explore. Jamie called up Google maps on her cell. The gray-green hills of a town with a definite dry season rose around commercial buildings and shops. They wouldn't see them until morning. A large gravel parking area spread out hundreds of feet around the docks. A glare of night lights lit the crowds of milling people and taxis waiting to pick up passengers. Trucks waited to receive the sacks of oranges and nuts and all the other goods.

As the clanking and jerking and engine noises settled them next to the pier, Tom asked Jamie if she would guard the forward deck while he watched the people going ashore. It took nearly an hour to empty the cabin and the deck. By eleven-thirty only, their crates remained.

The parking lot was almost empty. The ferry boat crew left also, including Julio, who shot a nasty look at Tom as he walked past, his fists balled. Tom gave him the finger. Something about the man brought out the coal miner in him. His hand went to his sore eye as he glanced at his watch. Time to get to work.

Captain Ricardo came out of the wheelhouse staircase. "All right, we'll get you off of my ship now." He took Tom's arm. "Do you have any protection?"

"Protection? Do you mean a gun? No."

"Come with me. I can't see you and that girl sitting on the dock all night without something to scare away bandits. The police won't be much help if you need them."

He opened a storage locker and reached behind a bolted down box of tools to draw out a machete. The curved blade was nearly two feet long and gleamed in the dim moonlight.

Tom took it to feel its weight. Heavier than he thought. "I don't know much about knife fighting."

"Here in Nicaragua most men can't afford a gun, but we all have machetes. The sight of it will serve to ward off any would be thieves."

"Thanks. I'll return it in the morning before the ferry leaves."

⸮ⸯ⸮ⸯ

Jamie crossed the forward deck to peek around the corner. What was Tom talking to the captain about? She gulped when she saw him waving a machete.

"The captain thinks we need some protection."

She chuckled. "Tell him it's too late because I'm already pregnant."

"Not that kind of protection." His big grin faded. "Let's get to work."

Jamie shuddered at the thought, but pushed the canvas aside and took hold of the first crate. "Wait. I have to turn around so I can be in front again." Awkward and hard, she thought, gritting her teeth as she walked, pushed forward by Tom at the other end of the crate, to the exit gate, down the plank to the gravel. This time she waited for Tom to lower his end before she dropped hers. She caught her breath walking back for the next one. Fifteen minutes later they had emptied the forward deck and started on the stern deck with no rest stop. She considered begging off as her muscles weakened. She didn't have enough breath to say it. *I can't stop. I signed up for this. Uncle James needs me.*

After they finished, she carried her pack, blanket, pillow, and the gym bag and flopped down on one of the boxes, while Tom thanked the captain for keeping watch for them and brought his stuff and the machete. Her legs and arms trembled. She leaned against the crates.

Tom sighed as he settled beside her. "Harder than it was this morning."

"Uh huh. Guess one of us will sleep on top of the boxes for a few hours while the other guards, and then change places. That's the plan, isn't it? Do you want to sleep or guard first?"

"Neither." He leaned back. "Guard first."

Jamie looked around at the glare. On one side of the loading lot, black lake water lapped quietly. A row of commercial buildings rose on the other side of a paved road parallel to the shore line. Two of them had lights on. Must be bars. "Look, I won't be able to sleep with these lights right overhead. I'll just stay up with you a while." She shifted her butt on the uncomfortable wood and put the pillow beneath her. "Those two bars are still open. Maybe I can go see if anyone in the bars knows where we can rent a boat in the morning. It won't take more than ten minutes."

Tom's hand rested on her knee. "Way too dangerous, milady. Your knight with his sword won't let you go alone into a bar filled with evil dragons in this strange foreign land." He picked up the machete and swung it.

Irked at his response, she pushed his other hand off her knee. "Who do you think you are? My father? Making me feel like I can't do anything because I'm a girl? I've pulled my weight so far, haven't I? If I walk into that bar and start asking questions, they will admire my guts, and answer me. I will leave before they get any ideas. I don't need your permission anyway." She stood up, daring him to answer, but not quite daring to walk toward the bars.

She was startled when he gripped her arm and forced her to sit again. She had gone too far. She shook his hand off. "Leave me alone. I'll go if I want to." Then she looked around to see if she'd been too loud and attracted attention. The lights on the ferry were out now. The captain must be sleeping. Not a single person was visible.

Tom humphed. "God, woman. You are a bundle. I can't let you take the risk of checking out those bars for a boat to rent at this time of night. You are right, though. That's the place to find one."

Clutching her hands together, she let him talk.

"I could go to that bar right across the street. Plenty of light. I saw two men go in there a couple of minutes ago. Maybe one of them has a boat. After all, this is a wharf. Look at all those boats moored along the beach. I can go over there and find out if someone can take us down the San Juan River tomorrow. You can stay here with the machete. You'll be all right for ten minutes."

He stopped mumbling and looked sideways at her.

She nodded. "I'll be fine. You go." He stood, took his copy of the contract with Estrella, and handed her the machete. She watched his familiar back walk away, comfortable that it would only be a few minutes. When he opened the door to the bar he turned and waved before he went in.

Jamie put the machete down on the boxes and walked around them. She didn't want her tired muscles to get stiff. She did a few squats and then picked up the machete and swung it around, pretending to swipe at an opponent. She put on a performance even though the empty gravel lot held no audience. Not even a car went by on the road.

In less than ten minutes, Tom came out of the bar with a short wobbly man. He gestured to the man to wait and ran across the lot to Jamie. "Hand me the gym bag. The old man, Arturo, agreed to take us to San Juan del Norte for twenty thousand." He dug out the bundles of cash. "He'll bring his boat around to tie up on the other side of this wharf with the ferry. I showed him our contract with the weights listed, and he can handle the weight. He's an old man and he's drunk, but the guys in the bar all vowed he knows the river better than anyone. It's a reasonable deal. I'll go with him to his boat. It's only a short way down the shore. I'll be back here in ten minutes with the boat. I think you'll be okay."

"Sounds good to me, but don't waste time. Go do it." He gave her a quick kiss on the cheek and ran back to the old man waiting outside the tavern. They lurched off together into the dark along the beach.

After he disappeared, she leaned back on the boxes again. *Don't go to sleep. You can stay awake for ten more minutes.* She forced herself to examine the dock area. At the far side a tourist information kiosk stood. A policeman had been standing guard outside the kiosk while the ferry unloaded. He wasn't visible now. The ferry dock stuck out at least ten meters into the lake water, with no boats on the opposite side of it, at least not tonight. Good. That would make it easy to load the crates in the morning. She got up and circled the boxes again to keep awake.

The lights went out.

"Uh!" she cried and fell back against the pile, as if hit. The glare was gone, and she couldn't see anything. Blind. In the dark. Her legs and arms trembled again. *Hurry up, Tom.*

They must turn the lights out at midnight. She fumbled around until her hand found the machete. How could she frighten anyone with it if they couldn't see it?

The low rumble of an engine stopped. She heard footsteps and voices whispering. She began to see the outline of her pile in the dim moonlight. She whirled to face the whispered comments.

The bulk of four men huddled together not five meters from her. Wide awake now, she raised the machete to fight them off.

"Help! Police!" she cried in Spanish. *Maybe that policeman will hear.* "Don't come near me. I'll cut you if you try to steal my crates. Keep away. My boyfriend is coming."

The four men came closer. "Oh yeah? Where is he now?"

"Julio!" A deep breath. Heat swarmed through her. For a long second, she didn't move. Then her sore leg muscles burst into action and crunched the gravel beneath her. She ran forward to meet them swinging her sword like an ancient warrior.

They stopped, but they didn't back up. *They aren't afraid of me because I'm a woman.* She saw that two of them had machetes that they raised to bring down on her if she got too close. She turned aside, afraid, but then cried out in anger, whirled around, and slashed Julio in the leg. He screamed and waved his hand to his men. "Get her!"

She ran onto the wharf and out toward the end of the dock. "*Ayuda!*" she screamed for help, her voice high and ragged. She swung wildly, looking for Tom and the boat he was bringing. She slowed to glance back. Two men were close behind her, one with a machete. Sweat ran down her arms. Tears burned her eyes. *They're going to catch me.*

A light came on in the wheelhouse of the ferry. She reached the railing at the end of the dock and turned, swinging at the two. The clang of metal meeting metal vibrated up her arm, shocking her.

The captain leaped over the ferry's railing down to the dock, landing on top of the two, with another machete swinging wildly. She heard cries of pain, but didn't know who was hurt. She couldn't swing her machete on the dark moving tangle of bodies.

She heard a motor behind her and saw Tom out of the corner of her eye standing on the bow of the boat, ready to leap onto the dock. She pounded on the captain and the two men tangled in front of her. She picked up the machete one had dropped and hacked at an arm she thought was not the captain's. When the thief screamed, she whacked his head with the flat of the machete and he dropped.

She pushed past the captain and the man he struggled with and ran toward shore, toward Tom, toward their pile of treasure. She realized she had a machete in each hand. She threw one to Tom after he jumped out of the boat. He leaped out of the way of the flying sword, swooped it up from the ground, and they raced together toward Julio and the other man. In the dim light of the moon they were carrying one of the small heavy boxes toward a waiting pickup.

"It's Julio," Jamie called.

"I'll take him," Tom called back. He raced ahead of her and called, "Julio."

Julio hesitated and Tom tackled him to the gravel lot, forcing him to drop the crate.

Jamie huffed and barreled into the man on the right, who lost his balance as Julio dropped the crate. He rolled upright out of her clutch, grabbed her arm to throw her aside, as he drew the machete from his belt. She backed away.

The old man who had brought the boat trotted up

with his own machete and began hacking left and right, shouting "Damn thieves! That's my cargo."

Tom screamed at Jamie, "Grab the box!"

She leaned over to pick up one side of the crate.

The two men from the dock slammed into her, knocking her away. She sat, trying to catch her breath from the shock to her stomach as Captain Ricardo flew past, flailing his machete.

The mass of men roiled on the ground. Julio shouted to his men to get the box and take it to the pickup, but the two with machetes had to defend themselves from Tom and Captain Ricardo.

The drunken old man raised his machete over his head with two hands and stumbled to the nearest target.

"Look out, Tom," she screamed.

The old man turned, and when he did, one of Julio's men raised his long knife straight into the swaying man's thigh. Jamie crawled through the gravel toward the falling man whose blood spouted as the dripping machete withdrew from his thigh. *He might die.*

The four armed men stopped their struggle as the old man fell to the ground. Jamie hated them all at the moment, soldiers who fought to kill, even Tom, even her. She bent over the bleeding man. The warm coppery smell of blood overwhelmed the sweaty smell of alcohol. It frightened her.

"Get the box, Juan," Julio yelled. "Let's get out of here."

The horde of men began to separate. Julio and Juan retreated slowly with the heavy crate to the back of the pickup. The other two thieves defended their retreat with their machetes, backing across the graveled tarmac. Tom and Ricardo followed them out of sight behind her. She could hear them, though, shouting at each other. The huffing and clanging sent shivers up her spine.

What can I do for this man? I'm not a doctor. Her hand crept to the spouting blood, spreading out over his thigh. She didn't want to touch it, but she had to see if she could stop the torrent. The slippery wetness rose through her fingers. She almost puked. She pressed just above where the blood welled. It slowed. He moaned and tried to roll away from her. She pressed harder. The bleeding stopped. *I need a tourniquet. I can't leave him.*

She glanced around. The battle turmoil had moved to the truck now. Tom was still on his feet, fighting. She ignored the worry for him.

Someone might see me, but I have to do it. She slipped off her tee shirt, unhooked her bra and slipped the tee back on. She pulled the bra tight around the man's upper thigh until she saw the bleeding stop. She wanted him to live, but he had lost so much. She needed a stick or bar of some kind to keep the bra tight enough. Her hands were tiring already.

She took a moment to look up at the battle. Everyone was shouting. She couldn't make out the words. Tom and Ricardo retreated, and the truck roared away. People had come out of the bar and stood watching, not interfering. Tom talked to them a minute and then headed back to her with Ricardo. Blood ran down his arm. They were discussing how to fight with a long knife.

Ricardo cradled his left arm with his right, his machete shoved through his belt. "You have to aim with the handle, not the tip of the blade," he explained.

Tom's machete swung at the same angle from his belt. Of the same height, muscles rippling, they walked like warriors, brothers-in-arms.

A hysterical giggle escaped her. How could she put tourniquets on three men? She stifled it, and studied their wounds as they approached. The captain's pinky was bleeding heavily. It will need stitches, she thought. The amount of blood running down Tom's arm was actually small. He just needed a wash and some antiseptic. She hoped that Ricardo or the man whose life she held in her bra would have some antiseptic. They probably had bottled water.

She would have to take care of them. "Hurry, I need a first aid kit and something to use to tighten this tourniquet. Bottled water too."

Chapter 5

Saving the Old Man

Tom stooped beside her. He didn't want to hear her orders now. He wanted to tell her what they had to do. It would be hard. Ricardo, with his shoulders slumped, still cradled his left hand with his right. Tom stood. His energy was running out. "Jamie, they almost got one of the small crates, but they left swearing to come back and take all of them."

Ricardo was explaining. "I sure did mistake what kind of man Julio is, willing to steal what he wants. He might come back before dawn to try again. You heard his threats."

"Can we stop them?"

"No. If they go to the police and complain that two men attacked them, trying to steal their crates of cargo, the police will see their wounds and they will come here to find you and the old man and the crates they are claiming. They'll put you in jail until it's sorted out."

"They wouldn't put us in jail because we have the contracts."

"Do not be sure about that. The police might expect a bribe."

Jamie wailed. "Is that why you were shouting? Dammit. How will we get the money for delivering the crates if we're in jail? We don't want to spend what we have to bribe the police." Her voice trailed off. "Uncle James will die. This man will die…"

"Be quiet, Jamie. Let the tourniquet loose for a couple of minutes. I have a plan." Tom laid his hand on her head, and she frowned up at him. What was she upset about? He had just saved her life. "We can't thank you enough, Ricardo. We'll be back in a few weeks to see you again after we finish this job. Right now we have to get you and Old Man Arturo to the local hospital. You need to have that fingertip sewn so it won't fester, and this man needs blood."

Arturo moaned a weak, "No." The wound welled blood freely again. "I won't go."

He tried to sit up, but Jamie shoved him down. "You're bleeding to death. Hold still." She tightened the tourniquet again.

Hard-hearted, Tom thought. Not like her. Her bra. A frisson of admiration for her ingenuity thrilled him. "I'll get something to use to tighten the tourniquet until we get him to the hospital."

The old man groaned a refusal again. Tom ignored him.

"Here's the plan. I'll go back to the bar and ask one of those witnesses to drive you to the hospital, Captain. You can send a medical van back here for Arturo. If you run into Julio and his men getting their wounds stitched before they talk to the police, you'll be able to tell the truth of what happened. After you're off to the hospital, I'll pay some men to help me lade the crates onto Arturo's boat. It would be hard to steal them from the boat. If Julio and his men do come back here with the police as they threatened, we'll just leave."

"Good plan. I will enjoy telling the police that the man I trusted to be my mate on the ferry is the true thief." He grinned. "Good fight we had. You have a real instinct for that machete. I'd shake your hand, Tom, if I could." He looked down at Jamie. "You take care of this man, young lady. He's strong and courageous and a good fighter."

Tom squirmed inside at the compliment. *During the fighting I panicked because I lost control and didn't want to get hurt. I don't deserve praise for staying alive.* "Let's go." He turned to Jamie. "Keep the tourniquet tight. I'll bring you a rod of some kind from the tavern."

She sat up straight glaring at him. *She likes giving orders, but not taking them, he thought.* Damn, he wanted her now, tonight. He could feel an inner strength settling over his uncertainties. Maybe the Indians portrayed by the statues felt that instinctive power before they became chiefs and donned the headdress animals. The animal part of him was growing.

In front of the bar, a half-dozen men stood talking

about the wild battle and the shouted threats. "Is it really diamonds in the crates?" one man whispered to Tom.

"No. It's really car parts for a new garage in San Juan del Norte."

The man looked disappointed, but elbowed his friend. "See, I told you."

Ricardo drooped even more and remained quiet. Tom saw he was pale in the light coming from the open door of the tavern. When he asked for someone to volunteer to take the ferry captain to the hospital, one man was proud to announce he had a car and he would do it right now. Tom's formal school-book Spanish was just right to tell the small crowd how grateful he was that the ferry captain had helped him, and actually saved two people's lives, not to mention cargo. "The people of San Carlos can be proud of Captain Ricardo, who is willing to fight like a soldier for truth and honesty." A little overboard, but true.

Ricardo rolled his eyes and grinned as he climbed into the car.

After he waved the car off, Tom called out to the owner of the *taverna*, "Free drinks and five dollars for anyone willing to help me load my crates onto Old Man Arturo's boat. I have a delivery to make." Three men were happy for the brief work. After giving the bar owner twenty dollars, he asked the man for a rod to tighten the tourniquet on the old man's leg. Tom laughed when he saw a plastic back scratcher, and told them that their friend, a regular at the tavern, was in bad shape. This might save his life.

When they got back to Jamie, she was grateful for the back scratcher. Tom had to pry her grip loose from the bra. She whimpered at the pain as she moved the fingers and rubbed her bloody knees.

The old man's friends crowded around him where he lay on the gravel. "Don't worry, the ferry captain is going to send the hospital ambulance."

Arturo's trembling fingers reached for his friend's shirt. "Don't let them take me. They will kill me in the hospital making me dry out. The last time they had me, I got the shakes for three days. Besides, I have to take these people down the river. They can't go by themselves. They need someone to show them the shallow parts, and the rapids, and how to hide from the border patrol."

Tom looked at Jamie who seemed as aghast as he.

"What do they know, a couple of tourists, about caimans?" the old man continued. "Or where to find food? That reminds me." He struggled to sit up. Jamie pushed him back down again. "Can one of you guys get a couple of bottles to last me to San Juan del Norte? I have the money right in my pocket, if this gal will let me get it." He patted the bulging pockets and his head lolled to the side.

Jamie slapped the man's hand. "Lie still, you old sot. If you keep moving, I'll loosen this tourniquet and you *will* die. I can't keep this tourniquet on you for two days. You have to get your leg sewn up, and you need a quart or two of blood."

Tom admired Jamie's performance. Arturo looked

shocked. So did his friends. However, the old man was right. How could they navigate the river? They didn't know the dangers. Rapids? Hiding from border patrols?

"I won't die. And if I do, I'll die happy." His friends nodded. "How about this bargain, miss? I'll get you started down the river to El Castillo, and you can leave me at the clinic where they don't know me, and you can pick me up on the way back."

"Can you do that, Jamie? Can you keep him alive long enough to get us halfway there? We really do need him." Guilt washed through Tom. He knew what Jamie was going to say.

"Tom, you can't just use him, knowing he might die. I can't believe you would even think of it."

It's the animal part of me, I guess. "I'm sorry. I don't see any other way to survive the trip down the river to save Uncle James." He was twisting her arm with that one. "Besides, I can alternate with you on the tourniquet. You know how to pilot the boat, and you can teach me."

One of Arturo's friends pleaded, "Take him with you, little lady. You don't know how awful it would be for him in the hospital here."

"Maybe we could save him this way, Jamie."

She seemed uncertain. Her eyes crinkled with worry, she peered around at the men. "Maybe. I don't know if I can do it. I'm not even sure how many minutes to leave the tourniquet off. He might live, but he might lose his leg." She rubbed her neck and loosened the bra. "I need some sleep."

"But will you do it?"

"Okay."

Tom sucked in his breath. He regretted this already. The man was going to die because of him. He wanted to survive and be successful in this mission to save her uncle, but not at the expense of Arturo's life.

Tom set them in motion. The men put Arturo on the black canvas. Tom took a corner and, with the other three, carried him to the open deck at the back of the boat. The old man whined as they hoisted him down to the deck. Tom saw tears begin and asked him where the hold was.

"What hold? This is a barge, not a cruise ship. Just tie your boxes to the rail. Cover them with canvas if you're worried about the rain." Arturo groaned and passed out when they lodged him in the right bunk of the cabin that covered the front half of the boat. Tom put Arturo's arm across his belly in the narrow bunk.

Jamie pushed in front of him, demanding he look for a first aid kit while she tightened the tourniquet again. He sent the men to haul the crates to the cargo deck. He found the first aid kit in a tiny cupboard under a single hot-plate, and pulled a chest from underneath the other bunk for Jamie to sit on. She gave him a grateful look and hugged his leg as he stood beside her. His irritation disappeared. He kissed the top of her head and headed out to arrange the crates.

With four of them working it only took a half hour to secure them as Arturo had directed. Tom glanced through the open door of the cabin.

Jamie stayed at the old man's side. He complained of

the pain when she loosened the tourniquet. "Dammit," she swore back at him. "You have to live."

Jamie will never forgive me if the old man dies.

∽∾

Jamie slipped her hand into Arturo's pocket for a wad of bills. His hand gripped her wrist to stop her, but loosened and fell back to his side. "Don't worry, old man, I'm taking just enough to get your liquor." She called to Tom. "Ask those guys to get Arturo's liquor, will you?"

"Sure, and some food and water for us too."

As soon as they had brought the food and drink, she suggested he lie down for a few hours.

"Julio and his men threatened to come back before dawn to get the diamonds. I should watch on deck."

"Don't worry, Tom. I'll hear their footsteps on the gravel if they come. Go to sleep now. Remember I had a nap this afternoon. I can wait up until dawn."

He didn't argue with her, but lay down on the bunk and slept.

She moved the chest nearer to the end of the bunk by the old man's feet, so it would be easy to reach the tourniquet on his thigh, and leaned against the bed post. She put her watch beside his leg on the bed and relaxed into a routine of fifteen minutes on and five minutes off. After the second round she jerked awake and saw that the blood had been running freely for ten minutes. Food would help her stay awake. She grabbed a sandwich and began the next round.

Two rounds later she heard a truck. It was nearly time to loosen anyway. She dropped the back scratcher and shook Tom awake. "I heard a motor stop. I'm going to check."

She reached the rail and before she could see anything across the parking lot Tom stepped in front of her.

"Get back in the cabin. They might have found a gun by now. Wake Arturo, so he can tell us where to go. If it is Julio's gang, we'll leave in the boat."

As she ran into the cabin a motor started up and began to cross the lot. "Arturo, you have to wake up."

"Huh?"

"That gang is coming back for the diamonds. We have to leave. Where's the key for the boat?"

"In my pocket underneath the cash. Right side." She jerked his leg over to get it out of his pants. "Be careful, woman."

"Hush, man. Can you hold the tourniquet?" She tightened it and handed the scratcher to him. "I'll be back in a minute."

"Is it them, Tom? Oh no…" The sliver of a moon hid behind a black clouded sky. Tom stood ready with his machete, one man against a gang. Large shapes appeared from the dark, but she couldn't make out how many. She took Tom's free hand. "Jump onto the wharf and untie the stern line then jump back on the boat." She'd never been on a boat with Tom. *He'll figure it out.* "Don't worry, it's easy. I'll pilot the boat. You handle the tourniquet as soon as we're far enough away."

She gave him a little push. "Go."

She ran through the cabin, saw that Arturo had dropped the tourniquet, and stopped to tighten it again. "You have to hold it or you'll die."

He opened his eyes and stared at her.

She ran out the front door of the cabin, leaped to the wharf to untie the forward line, and pulled the bow of the boat closer so she could jump back on. She raced into the wheelhouse. The motor started with a couple of coughs. She pushed in the choke and put it in reverse as it smoothed out. She backed slowly away.

The attackers ran onto the wharf. The first one to arrive, hardly a meter away, leaned over and grabbed the rail. Tom shouted and ran forward. He swung his machete at the hand on the rail. The man screamed. Jamie gave the barge some gas and its swift response pulled the wailing man into the water.

Julio's voice floated over the black water to her. "Murderers! I'll get those diamonds in El Castillo. You'll have to stop for gas."

As the boat moved away her breathing sharpened. She lightened her grip on the wheel and shook her hands to relieve the tension. When she thought she was far enough away from the shore she turned the engine off and floated, hoping the tide wouldn't pull her back to San Carlos. It was blessedly quiet for a moment. Little black wavelets lapped against the boat. Then she stepped to the rail and vomited. *I'm not cut out for this.*

She stepped into the cabin. Arturo whispered to Tom, "It's too tight, you fool. It hurts."

Jamie loosened it and twisted it as tight again as Tom

had. The old man was satisfied. "Listen, Arturo, you have to help us navigate the river. I have to find some place to tie up so I can sleep until dawn, and then we'll be off to El Castillo before Julio and his gang."

"I'll tell you where to go, but you have to do it, because this landlubber doesn't know anything. First you turn into the river and follow the shore by the light from the buildings. Stay about ten feet out until you pass beyond the town. You'll come to a large rock about ten meters high. Beyond it a creek flows in from the south. Turn into that creek. It's deep enough for the barge for the first ten meters. Go around the turn that's just after you enter, and anchor. You'll be safe until morning. Don't try to back out with the motor. Just use the poles alongside of the rail to keep clear of the banks. *Buena suerte.* Good luck." He closed his eyes.

Jamie muffled an okay, and Tom squeezed her. "I'll be in the wheelhouse, Tom, just a few feet away through that front door. We'll leave it open so we can talk if we want."

He nodded and let go of the tourniquet a moment to give her a kiss. It was so soft and warm. She didn't want to return to the wheelhouse, but she did.

She piloted the boat toward a light until she could just distinguish the shore and then turned east into the Rio San Juan. About fifteen minutes later she thought she saw the big black rock. When the blackness lessened a little, she turned off the motor and drifted, listening for the creek. When it got louder, she turned the motor on and very carefully turned into the creek. It was a bit wider than she had expected and when she got around the curve, she shut the engine off again, grabbed a hunk of tree branch leaning over the water and tied up the boat.

She mumbled, "Good night, Tom," as she fell into the other bunk. She hardly felt his goodnight kiss.

ာင

Tom sat beside the old man and leaned against the post. Fifteen minutes on and five minutes off by Jamie's watch. He started when Arturo began to talk.

"That's a pretty great gal you have. You treat her right and she'll stick by you. I know. I used to have a wife. She stuck with me even through the bad years." Arturo's eyes lowered to Tom's chest as he rambled on for several minutes, his voice weakening. He stopped talking and rolled over a bit. "I'm getting kind of dry. Hand me that bottle, will you?"

Tom handed him a bottle of water. "Drink this first, Arturo. You don't want to get dehydrated from losing so much blood."

"Yuk! Give me that bottle." Tom let him snatch the liquor bottle from his hands. He held the man up a bit until he got a few sips, and then took it away. He handed him the water bottle again and asked if he wanted a bite to eat.

"Maybe tomorrow."

As Arturo's eyes closed, Tom leaned back and began to tell the old man about him and Jamie. "She's the only girl I've ever loved. I met her in a sociology class last year. I admired how she dared to argue with the prof. We really didn't get to know each other until this backpacking trip." He looked at the old man. His breathing was deep and regular. "This summer together has driven me crazy." He shrugged. "She won't go to bed with me. She says she wants to, and acts like it too, but she won't give in because she's so angry with her father for paying me to protect her. Some protector I am." In his mind he replayed the swing of the machete and the man's scream. "She doesn't trust me."

Arturo chuckled, and then groaned. "How come my leg hurts when I laugh? Go on. You think I didn't hear you, but I did. I bet you convince her real soon, strapping young man that you are."

Tom snorted. "Hope you're right. I worry I'm not good enough for her. I probably killed someone tonight. Don't know what she'll think when she realizes what I did. Don't know what I think about myself." He looked down at Arturo. They stared, each intent on the other. The smelly old drunkard reached up to Tom's shoulder when he leaned over to adjust the tourniquet.

"A man does what he has to, and if she doesn't appreciate it, she isn't worth it. But a gal like her, intent on saving lives, will know that you wouldn't hurt someone unless you had to." His arm dropped back and he closed his eyes again.

Tom's voice dropped to a whisper. "I got so angry when that man tried to climb aboard. I don't know if I'll be able to handle the animal part of me." Arturo didn't answer. Tom drifted back to the time the bullet had ripped his leg. *I never got over that anger. That's why I hate guns. I'm afraid of what I might do.* He rolled the thoughts around for a while, and knew they were true.

It was time to begin the next round of the tourniquet. Arturo didn't wake up.

Chapter 6

Mamacita and the Alligator

The sun on her cheek through the small cabin window was warm enough to wake Jamie. She pushed aside the net and rose, wiping the sweat from her face with her sleeve. Ugh. She felt smelly and filthy. No washing since yesterday morning in Granada.

Tom leaned against the bed post at the old man's feet, his eyes closed. He stirred and loosened the tourniquet before he noticed her. He pushed aside the net that covered him and Arturo. "Hottest season of the year, isn't it?"

"Hey, ugly man, just look at you. Your arm covered with dried blood. Your shirt's been through two fights with a machete and is so stiff with sweat that I bet it won't bend. Dried blood all over our hands."

"Yuk."

"And look at Arturo. Now that's a problem. At least

he has the canvas under him to catch the blood. Let's do something. We have five minutes before tourniquet duty again."

Arturo rolled over slightly and opened his eyes. "Get this damned net off me and bring me the bucket tied to a rope on deck. Don't lower it into the water on the side where the spectacle caiman has her nest. Don't want to disturb her."

"Caiman?" Jamie asked.

"Kind of alligator. They make their nests in the dry season. Right now."

"Ummm," she answered, "Saw alligators in Florida."

Tom pulled her out the door. "Talk later. Wash now. Me first. Just throw the water over me. Look, that mass of weeds off the bow must be the nest." He threw the bucket over the other side. The water was only two feet below deck level. He leaned way over to pull up the bucket.

All of a sudden, Jamie tensed. "You idiot, don't lean so near the water. That caiman can jump out of the water and bite your hand off in a second."

Tom stepped back. "Is that it?" He pointed to the meter long gray streak that swam closer.

"Yep. That's its back that we see. See those two lumps sticking up at the front end? Those are its eyes."

Tom swung the bucket up and dumped the water on Jamie's head. She sputtered and squealed. With the rope in one hand he threw the bucket over the side again. It bumped on the head of the caiman which was right below him now, with its eyes staring at him from the baseball-sized lumps. The eyes rolled in the sockets, and the long snout moved back a few feet, leaving Tom room to sweep up another bucket. When he turned from the rail, Jamie was right in front of him.

"My turn." Her hands went under the bucket, lifted it the whole length of the rope, and dumped it on his head. He howled as the water ran down his face and in the moment he couldn't see, she snatched the rope from his hands. He started to laugh and, when she brought up the next bucketful, he grabbed one side of the handle. She giggled, pulling on the other side. They tugged lightly for a moment and both leaned on the rail, keeping tight hold of the handle.

Her hair was wet raven waves.

"I'll drop the bucket if you promise not to douse me again," she said.

"If I promise, you'll have to trust me." He dropped the bucket, wrapped his arms around her, engulfing her entire warm body, pinning her arms to her side.

She dropped the bucket. He let her loose and her hands crept under his wet shirt, running up his back. He lifted her chin and tipped her face up. He took a deep breath and kissed this wonderful girl. He rained little kisses all over her wet face. "Choose to be mine, Jamie. I want this forever. You're so brave, so determined. I don't ever want to live without you."

Jamie had tears running down her already wet cheeks. "Oh, Tom, you're such a good man. I don't want to wait another two weeks. What if I lost you?" Her arms pulled him tighter to her body.

With her breasts taut against his chest, his need for

her rose almost uncontrollably. He pushed her back to look at her. "You win the wet tee shirt contest." His hand slipped under her tee and held her breast, teasing the nipple with two fingers.

Her breath sucked in and her hands began to roam. Every fingertip raised heat on his skin, hardening him, heating him from the inside out. If he closed the cabin door, he could take her on the deck.

"Quit playing around out there," the old man called weakly, "and close this tourniquet before I bleed to death."

Tom wilted and stepped back from Jamie. She would have let him make love to her. It would have happened for sure.

Jamie's grip tightened on him for a moment, and she looked down. Then her hand rose to his cheek. She gave him a quick kiss and turned to Arturo.

Tom stooped to pick up the bucket and throw it over the rail. Frustration he could handle, but what if they *had* forgotten? Arturo might have died. He still might. Tom didn't want to figure out how to handle that kind of guilt. He hauled up the bucket, closed the cabin door, stripped naked, and washed his clothes. Since he had no soap he decided to change the water and do it again to get them clean. He washed his body and put the wet clothes back on. Maybe they would dry eventually. The heat and humidity would make it a slow process, though.

He opened the cabin door and put his hand on Jamie's shoulder. She held the tourniquet tight with one hand and reached up with the other to pat his. "I filled a fresh bucket for you to wash in. I'll take over until you're done, and then we'll work together on Arturo. He doesn't look well." His closed eyes and gray face worried Tom.

Jamie pointed to the still open wound. "Look. It's crusted a little at some edges, but it looks swollen and bright red here. After we wash up we had better go as fast as we can to El Castillo. Okay?"

He took her place. "Sure."

She took clean clothes out of her pack and left. As soon as he had a moment to loosen the bra, he changed to dry clothes also. He didn't want heat rash at a time like this.

Jamie came in with a bucket of water and set it next to Arturo. "We'll start at the top and work down. His whole body, whether he likes it or not. I'll look for some clean clothes."

"You're asking for trouble, babe."

"It needs to be done." She rummaged through cupboards and finally got to the chest Tom was sitting on. Sure enough, it had an almost clean change of clothes. She also had a wash cloth and a stiff towel. *If I get hurt, she'll take care of me, and if she gets hurt, I'll take care of her.* A moment of fear coursed through his abdomen. *I have to keep her safe from Julio and his men.*

⌘

As soon as Jamie started on Arturo's head, he began to moan and tried to push her hand away. After she had his hair and face and neck done, she changed the water.

No sign of the caiman. *Maybe she decided we aren't dangerous. Fat lot she knows.* Jamie's stomach twisted again, remembering last night. *How could we do that with the machetes? Kill and maim just for Uncle James? No, be honest—to save ourselves.*

She unbuttoned Arturo's shirt and washed down to his navel. He complained of the cold. She supposed it was the loss of blood. She'd cover his top half with the blanket from one of the cupboards. "Tom, I'm going to cut his shirt off. We can get him a new outfit in El Castillo. After I get it off, will you help me lift him a little so I can clean his back and maybe wipe up the canvas as much as possible?"

Tom nodded. "He's pretty much out of it, isn't he? Not a good sign."

"Yeah. I hope he stays out of it and doesn't struggle." She fetched the scissors from the first aid box and cut off his shirt. Arturo didn't complain until Tom let go of the tourniquet and raised him enough so that Jamie could clean his back and the black canvas.

Arturo didn't have the strength to howl or even struggle, but he occasionally shook his shoulders or kicked with his good leg. She got the cleaner shirt on him and Tom took up the scratcher again, while she changed the water.

As weak as he was, when she started to remove his pants his eyes flew open. "What are you doing, woman? Can't you leave a sick man alone?"

"I have to clean you. I'm trying to prevent infection. Remember, I'm a nurse." She glanced at Tom after she told this lie that she hoped would calm the old man. Tom was chuckling.

"Just wait, Tom. After I finish what I can, you can wash his private parts."

Tom stopped chuckling. She was able to roll Arturo on his side and wash his buttocks and the top part of his legs. They and the canvas, stiff with dried blood, took a lot of work and she had to change water halfway through.

Arturo kept up his weak stream of complaints. "I want my bottle before I get the shakes. What's the use of keeping me alive if I can't have my bottle?"

She lifted him and gave him a few swigs, promising he could have more later. Then she rolled him over to his other side and cleaned some more. She made Tom move over so she could wash the old man's calves. Then there was nothing left except his private parts and the wound itself. She brought a new bucket of water and handed the cloth to Tom. He looked horrified, but took the cloth.

The moment he started to work Arturo opened his eyes and roared. It was weak, but understandable. "Don't touch me! What kind of man are you?"

Tom jumped back. The electric shock of accusation turned him red. He tossed the cloth to her. "I'm not doing this."

Arturo opened his eyes long enough to say, "If anyone has to do it, let it be you, little lady. I might even enjoy it."

Jamie's cheeks warmed. She rolled her eyes at Tom and proceeded to work. It would have been easier with soap, but the old man might have liked it too much. Actually, it seemed to calm him a bit. She washed off around the wound as well as she could without touching it.

"Arturo, can you wake up? I need to talk to you before we finish."

"I'm tired. I don't know if I can stay awake."

"I know. You've lost so much blood." She kissed him on the forehead, glad that he didn't smell anymore.

He gave her a little smile.

She held his hand. "Captain Arturo. We have to leave this cozy safe haven and cruise down the river to El Castillo so we can get you sewn up, and get you some blood. We need to move fast. Tell us what problems we might have. Any shallows? What about those police we have to watch out for?"

"Lady." He paused for a moment. "Jamie, isn't it?"

"Yes."

"Jamie, stay in the middle." He breathed. "Unless you see a small sandy island. Keep to the other side." He breathed. "If the river curves to the left stay on the left. If the river curves to the right stay on the right." He breathed. "No police inspection stations until the river hits the border of Costa Rica. After El Castillo." He breathed. "Enjoy the animals, and birds. Don't get in the water." He breathed again and squeezed her hand. "Last and most important. Look for an island completely covered with caimans of different sizes and kinds. Go around the bend after it, and look for a small dock on the right with a stairway up the cliff wall to the farm at the top." He stopped for a moment and closed his eyes. Before she could panic he took a deep breath and began again. "Go up the steps and talk to Marcella. She'll give you lunch and some potions. She's good. That's all."

"Wait, Captain. I have to warn you. I'm going to pour some of your whiskey on your wound to kill some of the germs. It will hurt, but I think I have to do it. Will you forgive me?"

He smiled with his eyes closed. "Only if you kiss me goodnight after."

"Let go, Tom." She pulled the dirty bra from around his leg. She picked up the bottle and poured it carefully on the wound before he changed his mind.

He squealed as the pain of the alcohol cauterizing the edges of his wound set in. The squeal turned to "Ah, ah, aaah. Stop burning." His panting slowed.

"I'm so sorry, old man," she whispered.

She took the bra and washed it as thoroughly as possible without soap, wrung it out as much as possible, and slipped it back around his leg. Arturo's breathing slowed more. Maybe he was unconscious.

Jamie looked at Tom. She wanted a hug from him, and, though he was looking at her, he had to hold onto the tourniquet.

He shook his head. "You are magnificent."

The next two hours were a strange mix of hurrying and slowing. Jamie gripped the wheel, rigid with the tension of constantly watching for shallows. If the barge stuck in the sand they would be dangerously delayed. Once in a while she called Tom to use the pole to check the depth. They passed a few short docks on the south side of the river, and twice she waved at a small motorboat going the other way.

The birds standing majestically on sandbars, a dozen different combinations of white, gray and black, distracted her. The small ones squawked as they swam out of the way. The large ones lifted their great wings and gracefully flew to branches on the jungle trees rising on both sides of the river.

Squawks and flaps echoed between the brown muddy cliffs, five to ten meters high and topped by huge trees. Green bushes and vines in numerous shades of emerald covered everything, varied only slightly by crimson or yellow flowers. Occasionally, Jamie saw a flash of red or blue, or heard the splash of a caiman's tail as it slid off a sandbar.

She saw no houses or roads along the banks. She did see several signs advertising lodges, with arrows pointing up the large creeks that flowed into the San Juan. The river *was* the road. More small motor boats passed the barge on the way to San Carlos. She chatted with two backpackers in rented kayaks going down river. They were heading to one of the docks on the south side of the river that led up to a small village.

"How many villages on the river?" Jamie asked.

"Only this one between here and El Castillo. The north side is all jungle preserve."

When she saw the large sandbar covered with, she guessed, fifty or so caimans, large and small, she called, "Tom, come and see this." She kept as far to the right of the sandbar as she could.

Tom whistled. "No wonder Arturo told us to stay out of the water. Look at the size of that one on the point of the bar. It must be five or six meters. Think of how many fish must be in the river to keep them all fed." He leaned over the bow. "I can't see anything in the water. It's all black."

Jamie rounded the next bend and spotted the short dock on the south side, with stairs rising to the top of the cliff through vines and weeds. She saw only trees. She pulled in slowly to the pier and turned off the motor. Tom wielded the pole so they wouldn't ground.

He abandoned the pole about four feet from the cliff, jumped onto the dock and tied the boat. "I'll go up first, Jamie. All we know is that a woman with potions lives at the top. If it seems safe, I'll come back down and you can go up. Okay?"

"Yes." She appreciated his care, but she would have liked to go up the steep stairs to see what was at the top.

It was a long half-hour until he clambered down the stairs, chewing a piece of flatbread. A skinny middle-aged woman followed him, carrying a sack. Jamie barely kept herself from staring at her. She was so beautiful, clearly Indian, with a large portion of oriental yellowing her skin and slanting her black eyes. Jamie had heard in her anthropology classes that the general idea of the early history of the Americas was that the natives discovered by Columbus had arrived more than 15,000 years ago. Geneticists had confirmed that probably the Chinese sailed to the Americas a century before Columbus and left colonies here. It might be true, she thought.

"This is Marcella. She prefers Mamacita. Remember Arturo said she has potions? She has some in her pack." He pointed to her capacious bag.

"Hello, Mamacita. Can your potions help Captain Arturo?"

"I hope so," Mamacita said in a soft, whispery voice. "I've known him for many years. He has always been kind and generous to me. Your Tom explained to me that he helped fight off some robbers in San Juan. Please let me see him. I want him to live." She looked down, as if embarrassed.

"That would be wonderful. I hope it won't take long. We're hurrying to El Castillo. They have a small clinic where they can sew him up and give him a blood transfusion and an antibiotic. I think he's unconscious."

Jamie led her to the old man. Mamacita sucked in her breath and shook her head when she saw his state. "You are right to be worried. He is infected already." She pointed out the redness and explained that the tissue felt pulpy when she put her fingers on it.

Jamie hoped her hands were clean.

"I have some ancient knowledge of plants. Will you allow me to put a poultice on his wound? It will help it to heal."

Jamie hesitated. Should she trust her? "All right. Arturo says you are good with potions."

"I have a garden where I grow medicinal plants. I learned about them from my mother and grandmother. I hope these will be some help. I just picked them." She took out a handful of oval shaped leaves with points on the end. "This plant is called 'tail of the rat' because the flower is on the end of a rat-like tail. My grandmother got the plant from some island up north." She spread the leaves out over the slash in his leg. "Now I'll put a warm poultice on his wound. It's just the mashed pulp of a cactus plant with a little salt. The plant looks like this." She took out a thick leaf, holding it carefully between the long spines. "You can mash the leaf to get the pulp out and use it to wash your hair. Here."

Jamie took it carefully and handed it to Tom to put on the counter.

"This looks like prickly pear with spines."

Mamacita took a mason jar full of warm yellow mash, spread it under the leaves, and covered it with a cloth which she loosely tied around the old man's leg. "Later this afternoon, warm the rest of it on his hotplate, scrape off the old poultice, put this on, and retie the cloth. You can do this?"

"Sure. I know enough about cooking to warm something in a pot."

"Then let me give you some other plants to help you and send you on your way. You need to hurry to El Castillo to get a transfusion. Probably several pints. I hope they have enough." She reached into her voluminous bag and came out with some wavy leaves.

"That looks like plantain," Jamie exclaimed. "I used to help my mother weed the garden at home when I was little."

Mamacita gave a soft laugh. "Good. Make a tea of this and add a bit of salt and mint. It's good for shock, and will also get some liquid in him. Wake him up if you can and make him drink the whole thing. Do it as often as he will let you." She brought out several more packets of leaves in ordinary plastic bags. "If he gets a fever or vomits, a tea made with this fit-weed will help. These last two bags are for you and Tom. I hope you don't need them. You know the closer you get to the coast the worse the mosquitoes get. This is the dry season, but it still rains here about every other day. It will rain this afternoon. Hang this long stem with leaves and flowers over the beds. It will keep the mosquitoes away. Use this bit of cream on any bites you get. Last I have a piece of a vine that helps with snake bite. You never know when a snake might fall from a tree along the edge of the river. Even in town snakes bite people. These tri-lobed leaves make a tea that helps, and this peculiar flower can be mashed for a poultice to draw the venom out of the bite."

Jamie shivered. "Do you really think we need all that? Is it that dangerous on this river?"

Again the soft laugh. "Tom told me you're going to the Amazon. You might need it."

Tom was digging in one of the cupboards for Arturo's cash. He shoved a large packet of it toward Mamacita's hand. "We'll stop on the way back if we have time, to visit some more. You will be able to see if Arturo survived." Mamacita pushed the cash back, but Tom put it in her bag anyway.

He was so good.

"Thank you for your help, Mamacita," Jamie said. "Maybe Arturo will live because of you."

Mamacita had calmed her fears that this man would die and that she would be responsible. Jamie gave her a hug. She left the tourniquet to walk with her to the dock. "I hope on the way back I will get to see your fascinating garden."

Mamacita reached into her bag and handed Jamie another mason jar. "Rice and beans for your lunch." She started up the steep steps.

Jamie watched her for a moment, hopeful, and almost content. Tom was back by the crates leaning over to check the way back into the center stream of the river. Smiling at his careful attention to details, she untied the boat and stepped up to the deck.

As she shifted her weight to the foot on the deck it tipped up. She flailed her arms in the air and saw a large alligator tail disappearing under the boat. The boat shifted away from the dock.

Her heart thudded and she whimpered. She was falling into the water.

She hit her head on the dock. The water closed over her head. She felt dull for a moment and hung in the water. Then she remembered the alligator and needed to breathe. She lashed out with her feet to move up. Her sandal slipped off and her foot hit the lumpy alligator skin. She knew it was the alligator and waited for his bite. Her head broke water and she gasped and reached for a post of the dock, screaming. A fish brushed her leg and hyped her panic. "Help! Tom!" He was there, pulling her out of the water to get a knee on the dock and drag her other leg up.

A huge head rose out of the water, and the snap of teeth filled the air. She clung to Tom's knee and he dragged her into his arms.

Mamacita was screaming above them, "Are you all right? Did he bite you?"

"She's okay," Tom called. Jamie lay in his arms, still gasping.

Tears ran down her face. She couldn't stop trembling. *It almost got me. Tom saved me. Again.* She wanted to stay in this hug forever.

∞∞∞

Tom squeezed her tight against his chest. "You're okay. You're okay," he mumbled several times, rocking her, rubbing her head.

He looked up. The barge was drifting away. He pried Jamie's hand away from his shirt as she looked up at him, questioning with her eyes. "The boat's floating away!" He stood. "Mamacita, do you have a boat hook?"

"Yes, it's on the side of the dock, on your right side. Are you sure she's all right?"

Tom got the hook, walked to the end of the short dock. The pole was just long enough to hook the drifting barge. He pulled the heavy craft in, wrapped the rope twice around a post and turned back to Jamie. Mamacita was holding her.

"I hit my head on the dock when I fell. I guess that's why I'm still kind of groggy."

Mamacita studied her eyes. "You'll be all right. I

don't think you have a concussion. Check with a medic when you get to El Castillo. You better get going now." She pulled Jamie to her feet and handed her over to Tom. "Take care of her."

He nodded and they boarded the barge. "Can you take the wheel and get us going?"

"Yes, I'm okay."

Tom sat down with the tourniquet and watched her through the door to the wheelhouse. The hurrying and slowing began again.

The twice-weekly ferry from San Carlos passed them. It was ten meters long, and had four seats across with a narrow middle aisle. The locals and tourists who filled the boat waved at them as they passed "What time will you get to El Castillo?" Jamie called out.

"Four o'clock if we don't have too many stops along the way for the locals."

"Thanks. I think I'll follow you. I don't know the river very well."

"Sure," the pilot called back.

Tom had a tourniquet break and joined her in the wheel house. "You're still okay?"

"Fine, except for the lump on my head." She paused, slumped, and then looked up at him, flashing him her blue eyes. "Tom, this is hard to say. I'm sorry I didn't trust you because my dad paid you to protect me this summer. It doesn't matter anymore. You saved my life twice. I'll always trust you. I know that I'll always love you."

She didn't blink or turn away. She really meant it.

His heart raced. "Will you still feel that way if I fail you sometime? I can't be perfect, Jamie, but I want to be good enough for you." He waited, not breathing.

He was taken aback when she laughed. He hadn't expected her to laugh at this serious stuff. She let go of the wheel and flung her arms around him. "You're not perfect, Tom. Sometimes you want to control me, like my father. I'm not perfect either. Sometimes I try to tell you what to do. Sometimes I don't listen. Just the same, I know now that you will take care of me as best you can, and I want the chance to do that for you." She looked up at him, her eyes crinkled by her big grin. "Will you marry me, Thomas Lee Kirk?"

He felt his knees weaken. He burst out in laughter, and euphoria made him reach for her. He lifted her and swung her around, while she giggled. He pulled her close and hugged her. Raising his arm to the sky he shouted, "Yes!" People in the boat ahead turned around to look at them. "She wants to marry me," he called to them, sparking their laughter and congratulations. He hugged her close. "I love you now, Jamie Ann Patrick, and I will always love you."

For a long moment he clung to her, reveling in the warmth of her arms around him. A whisper of current turned the bow of the boat and he reached for the wheel.

"Now that I've caught you, I'm going to tell you what to do" she said.

He laughed again, full of new energy. "Anything, darling, anything."

"Take the wheel and follow the ferry in front of us. If

it stops to pick up or let off a local, don't follow it to the dock. Just put the engine in neutral like this." She showed him.

"Sure, I can do that. It's not much different than driving a car."

"The current can complicate things. Call me if you need help. I can do the tourniquet duty and also make the tea and the poultice in between."

"Okay." He couldn't stop smiling. She stepped through the door into the cabin and he noticed her bare foot. "I'll buy you some sandals at El Castillo."

"Oh. My head is so full of other things I forgot about it. I'll put my boots on."

He turned to the wheel. It was easier than he thought. He tried different speeds and different directions until he got the feel of it.

He settled back in the chair and wondered what it would be like to fish. Peaceful. A deep satisfaction let his mind wander. He began to count the various species of birds, calling them out to Jamie behind him. "When we have a house someday, let's put a small aviary in the garden."

"And we can have a plot of medicinal plants," she replied, evidently thinking of the future as he was. His tuneless whistling turned into an effort to whistle "Yankee Doodle." Fruitless. He sang it instead.

The ferry ahead began to turn into a dock. He put the engine in neutral and walked to the back of the barge through the cabin, giving Jamie a pat on the bottom as he passed. "I'll throw out the anchor so we don't drift past the ferry."

"It's a heavy one with six flukes. It will probably work well in this sand."

He walked past the crates toward the stern. "Jeez, Jamie, when the caiman tipped the boat I fell against the crates and one of the small ones fell off the pile and spilled open. I didn't see it because you were screaming. We were in such a hurry last night we didn't tie them well enough."

Chapter 7

Guns and Rocket Launchers

Tom hurried to the anchor, picked up the fifty-pound hunk of metal, and shot-putted it over the port rail. Seven meters of chain trailed after. Thank god for his weight lifting.

He knelt beside the turned over wooden box. A mixture of powder and stones lay on the deck between the crate and the lid. He fingered the stones, wondering if these small roundish gray things were raw diamonds. He couldn't check Wikipedia on Jamie's phone because no Wi-Fi service penetrated this part of third-world Nicaragua. Maybe El Castillo would have a tower. San Juan del Norte surely would.

He righted the box and scratched the tightly packed stones and grit. *If these are raw diamonds what does Julio think he's going to do with them? He'd have to find some expert to polish and cut them, and that person was unlikely to be in this country. They'd arrest him right away. He might be able to get ransom money for the diamonds, I suppose.*

Tom quit thinking about Julio and ran his hand around the upside down cone shaped hole to measure its size. He had to put the stones back into the box and pack them tightly. His fingertip touched something that felt like plastic at the bottom of the hole. Pulling his hand out he peered inside. It was black at the bottom of the hole, not gray. He felt again. It wasn't grit.

We're in trouble. "Jamie," he yelled, running into the cabin. "Where's my pack? I need my knife."

"What's going on?" she asked. She untied the string around the poultice on Arturo's leg.

Tom took her by the shoulders and turned her to look at him. "You have to come and see."

She stirred the pot on the hotplate warming the mashed goo from the cactus. "Okay. Just for a minute."

Tom grabbed his pack and pulled her out the door to the spilled diamonds. "Put your hand in the hole in the box."

She stooped and put a finger in. "Oh." She fell back on her butt. "That's not diamonds. That's not good."

"Scrape those raw diamonds together while I dig out what's in the box." It took him a couple of minutes to pry out the packed stones still in the box. A black plastic bag filled it to the edges. He dumped it out and two packages fell with a heavy thunk onto the deck. "It's too heavy to be cocaine."

"But what is it? If we open the packages to look at it

the man we're delivering to will know that we've been in the crates. Estrella might not give us our money. Maybe we should just put the box back together and forget it." She glanced behind her at the cabin. "Listen, I have to get back to Arturo. He's still bleeding slowly. I have to get that tea into him."

"You're probably right. Besides, the ferry is backing away. I have to get back at the wheel."

Jamie disappeared into the dark of the cabin.

Tom glanced at the dimming sky. Rain soon. He scooped up the stones and grit from the deck and threw them in the box. He could pack them tight later. He started to crank up the anchor, but grew impatient and leaned over the rail to pull it out of the sand. It let loose with a final yank and he quickly wound it up. He hurried through the cabin into the wheelhouse, brushing past Jamie who was shaking Arturo, trying to wake him.

She propped him up a little. "I'll just pour a little down his throat to see if that will wake him."

As he put the motor in gear to follow the ferry, Tom heard the old man coughing and sputtering. Live, man, live, he thought. The next few minutes he listened to Arturo's weak complaints and his demands for liquor. Jamie prevailed and got a whole cup of the brew into him.

The tourniquet had been loose for at least ten minutes. "Arturo, I'll let you sleep now, but in twenty minutes you're going to drink another cup of tea."

The old man's moan trailed off.

Finally, quiet. Rain began a gentle drum on the canvas over the wheel house. The birds stood silent on the sandbars or in the jungle trees, which seemed closer overhead. Tom pondered his moral dilemma.

I have to see what's in those crates. It must be illegal or they wouldn't have hidden it. I can't turn the stuff over to the border guards up ahead. We'll end up in jail and the Amazon Indians will kill Uncle James. His chest tightened. *I probably killed that man whose hand I chopped off last night.* He twisted in his chair. *I can't take it back. It will be hard to live with. Jamie hasn't thought about it yet. She's too involved with saving the old man and Uncle James.* An irregular sigh escaped. *I was protecting us. Julio would have killed us.*

The ferry rounded a bend out of sight. Tom followed and saw a long straight stretch ahead.

I'm only justifying what I did. I could have done something else. Denial. I don't like that I killed somebody, no matter the reason. I enjoyed the fighting. What kind of man am I? I have to find out what's in those boxes.

He called out to the ferry ahead. "How long is this straight stretch of the river?"

"About fifteen minutes," the pilot answered.

"Any stops?"

"Only one."

Tom thanked him, put the engine in neutral, ran through the cabin to the stern and shot-putted the anchor into the water again. He had to see.

"What?" Jamie called,

"I'm going to look in the boxes." He pried up the lid of one of the big ones and took out a cylinder. He unscrewed the cap. Raw diamonds. Was that all it held? He scraped at the stones. Two inches down his knife hit something hard. He scraped out the diamonds on each side of it and found a metal tube covered in clear shrink-wrap.

The barrel of a gun. He scraped more out until he could turn it over and get the gun out. A Kalashnikov. He didn't know clearly what they looked like, but it seemed similar to the ones the guards had toted in front of the bank—and in front of Estrella's warehouse. He dropped it as if it were burning. The rain beat on his head. He'd better close the lid before the clay got too wet.

He opened one of the two biggest crates. No cylinders, just a crusty packed layer of diamond core. He scraped enough off to see another shrink-wrapped package. Tugging at it he spilled clay grit and diamonds all over the deck. It took a minute to figure out what it was. A long six-inch wide barrel flared at the end like a trumpet. In the center was a large lump of metal parts with a trigger, and a handle farther down the barrel. He lifted the heavy thing and it landed on his shoulder. The realization stunned him. A rocket launcher! He lifted it enough to examine the other end. There were two holes for ammunition.

We have to get out of this. Without going to jail.

He shuddered and raised the weight of the killing machine from his shoulder back to the crate. He crumpled and sat on the deck in the midst of the scattered diamonds, his face in his hands for a moment. They were doomed. "Jamie," he called.

ୡୡ

"Can it wait?" Jamie answered.

"Not really."

She put the tea down, leaving her cranky patient. Tom sat in the drizzle in the middle of clay grit. He really looked upset. She put out a hand to help him up, not that he needed it. "What did you find?"

"The eight boxes have Kalashnikovs in them. The small boxes have ammunition. The two large boxes have rocket launchers in them."

Her hand flew to her throat. "Oh my god, oh my god," she wailed, walking in a tight circle. "What'll we do?" She leaned into him and felt the grit on his pants. She brushed it off. "First let's get this clay off the deck before the rain soaks it."

A thin smile crossed his face. "Yeah, get it back into the crate before it hardens. We don't want the guy in San Juan del Norte to suspect we've been in the boxes. We probably wouldn't get paid."

"And Uncle James…" Her throat tightened again and she slumped against the rail. "We should turn the guns over to the first border police post we come to after El Castillo, but they'll put us in jail while they figure out who's doing what." Tears of frustration burst from her eyes. She turned and pounded the rail. "All these people dying—my uncle, Arturo, and that guy whose hand you chopped off. And all of the people the guns will kill. Somebody has to stop Estrella and whoever else is responsible."

Tom's arms hugged her from behind. "Shh, shh. I have an idea. What if we deliver the goods and they don't suspect we know. It will take several days for the shipment to arrive in New York. We can call the US government, the FBI probably, or the coast guard, and tell them about the smuggled guns. We'll have time to go back to Estrella, get the money and be on our way to Ecuador before our government goes after him. What do you think?"

She turned in his arms and squeezed him. "Maybe it will work. We'll save lives and stay out of jail." She wiped her eyes. "I'd better get that tea into Arturo." She blew him a kiss as she headed into the cabin.

❦⚭❧

Tom took a deep breath. "All right," he said and scooped up as much of the clay debris as he could. Then he hauled up the anchor. Jeez, it was heavy. He had to catch up to the ferry. Only an hour to El Castillo.

Uh oh. Julio threatened to catch us at El Castillo and get the diamonds. He hollered it right in my face.

Tom called out to the ferry boat when he reached it. "How many stops are there at El Castillo?"

"Two," a guy in the back of the boat answered. "One around the bend just before the main stop where we get off. It's mainly for getting gas and loading large supplies."

"Can you tell me about it?"

"Sure. They only use it a couple of times a week. There's a road up the bank that goes to the back of the old hotel."

Great. I can sneak into town without Julio seeing us. He probably passed us while we were in the estuary this morning. "Thanks. Let me know when we get close to it so I can pull in."

The rain petered out. If it stayed cloudy it would get dark early, about six maybe. They wouldn't have much time. It was almost four when the passenger from the ferry called, "It's the next dock."

"We're almost at the landing, Jamie. You'd better take over to pull into the dock. I might not slow the barge fast enough. I'll take over the tourniquet. Okay?"

"Sure. He's really out now. We need that blood fast."

"Dock the ship and we'll talk about how to go about it."

She's frowning. Why doesn't she like that?

He watched her dock the barge through the doorway. After she had tied up at the long pier, she came back and sat, stiff and straight, on the bunk opposite him.

"I'll go up first to find out if Julio's gang is here. Then I'll find the hospital and get someone to bring blood down here. He's a dead weight, and I won't be able to carry him up the hill."

"So you think I should stay here and hold the tourniquet while you take care of everything."

"Don't you want me to?"

"You assume you don't need me. You don't even know what blood type Arturo is. How are you going to bring the right type? And why not get an ambulance down here to take him to the hospital?" Her voice was rising.

She's really mad. "I'm sorry. I thought you wanted me to take care of things, protect you." *I've been following her around all summer, doing whatever she wants, and now when she needs my help, she expects me to follow her orders like a puppy dog.* It burst out of his mouth. "You can't order me around. I need to keep you safe." He let go, yelling, "I'm not your puppy dog!"

She stood, leaning over him, and hollered in his ear. "Well, I'm not yours!"

He winced. "Can't we compromise?"

She straightened and paced up and down like a caged tiger. "How?"

His mind raced. "We can both leave for twenty minutes if we take the bra off and retie it in a knot tight enough to keep the wound from leaking. We'll just cut the bra off when one of us gets back here with blood."

"That's good. Let the tourniquet loose for a few minutes now before we tie it tight. I'll go to the hospital and see how much blood they have. It's O, the most common type. I'll bring back an ambulance." She stopped. Her blue eyes challenged his. "What will you do?"

He let go of the bra tourniquet and tossed it on the counter. "I need to find out if Julio is here. The town is small. If they're outside, I should be able to find them in ten minutes. If I see them, I will back away. We don't want them to know we're here. Then I'll go to the hardware store for some nails and a hammer to use on those crates and come back to the boat." He stood and took her by the shoulders returning her stare. "I trust you to take care. Keep watch on your way to the hospital."

"I'll have to trust you to find out if Julio is here." Jamie patted Arturo on the head. "You concentrate on living, old man. We still need you." She leaned down and planted a kiss on his forehead. "I hope he doesn't lose his leg. Tie it tight, Tom. Let's go."

Freed from the barge and the worry of finding blood, Tom vaulted over the rail to the dock and gave a hand to Jamie. "We have to hurry, babe." He ran up the hill with Jamie right behind.

They jogged the quarter mile to the hotel, which was a huge dark wood building three stories high, surrounded by trees and flowering red azaleas. Tom thought that nobody could see them, except the man carrying out garbage. They pulled up and Jamie asked where the hospital was.

"You mean the clinic? You just passed it. It's that white building. That's the back of it."

Jamie looked uneasy with her eyes squinted. "I didn't see any ambulance. Well, I'm off." She kissed him and ran.

"Have you seen any unusual people around town today? I mean, not tourists?" he asked the garbage man.

"No. What are you looking for? I have to get back to work."

"Where's the hardware store?"

"About two blocks over, right next to the stairs up to the castle."

Tom nodded and walked around the side of the famous hotel toward the street in front, checking the side streets, looking for Julio or Juan, the two he could recognize. He kept to the left and worked his way up the two blocks toward the cliff above the river. A green plaza opened in front of him. Fifteen or twenty tourists and locals spilled into the plaza from a set of stairs. He recognized one from the ferry boat. The dock must be down those stairs.

He hung back, not stepping into the plaza, and watched the locals disappear quickly with their packages. The tourists stood around for a while, deciding where to go. Some headed to the hotel with its restaurant, and some headed to the east end of the plaza toward the stairs up to the castle. It was really a fort, looking over the river, protecting the Spaniards from the British a hundred years ago. Too bad he wouldn't get to explore it.

As the crowd in the plaza dwindled, Tom spotted a man leaning on the fence in front of the bushes lining the edge of the cliff. He was watching up the river to the west. He might be one of Julio's men, watching for the barge. Tom didn't recognize him, so he waited, still, in the shadow of the building before the plaza.

He must not be able to see the barge around the bend. Good. They don't know we're here. We'll be safe if no one spots me. I think I rather enjoy slinking around like a spy. So far, so good. He waited, aching inside. He remembered Jamie screaming into his ear. He didn't treat her like a puppy dog.

He didn't want to control her. He wanted to protect her, keep her safe. Part of him knew he was justifying his own anger. *What if she changes her mind? It's just that she's so...volatile. What if I can't live the rest of my life with her?*

Tom moved back one block from the plaza and headed west toward the steps to the castle and the hardware store next to it. He loitered beside the hardware and watched the man stationed at the top of the stairs. When he turned his back, Tom quickly slipped into the square and into the *fereteria*, the hardware store. What if Julio was in the store? Tom cautiously cased the aisles before relaxing enough to purchase nails, a hammer, a pair of sandals and two rain slickers. He found a pair of jeans and a shirt for Arturo.

At the screen door, he surveyed the square to the left for a moment. The guy watching upstream for the barge had left his post and a policeman replaced him. Tom turned right and saw Julio and his gang not three meters from him at the stairs. He jerked backward, bumping the clerk behind him.

"You seem very nervous, sir. Perhaps you are worried about that policeman? I don't want any trouble. Please leave."

Julio and his men were mounting the stairs to the castle. Tom doubted they wanted to take a tour. "Sir, I haven't done anything wrong." He pointed to Julio and his men. "Those men are not tourists. Why are they going up to the castle?"

"I don't know, sir. Please leave."

"Right." As soon as Julio was out of sight, Tom hurried out the door down the hill to the ship. *Spying is a boring game anyway. Sneaking around is cowardly.*

Did she find a doctor? He had a vision of a man cutting off Jamie's bra and throwing it on the counter. He remembered his hands on her breasts. He wanted her to be his.

Chapter 8

Overboard into the Rapids

Jamie heard Tom's boots clunk onto the deck and she rushed out of the cabin to him. "Is everything all right? You took so long." She hesitated to hug him, still stewing inside about the way he had treated her. She didn't like having to get his permission for what she wanted to do.

"Yep. Julio is up by the castle, but he didn't see me. He has men watching for us up by the castle, and by the stairs down to the dock. I got the hammer and nails, and a couple of slickers for us and sandals for you. The fereteria even had clothes for Arturo. How's the old man?"

"Alive, but still not great. Did you see the pickup by the dock? No ambulance. The hospital is only a clinic, with a physician's assistant instead of a real doctor. He only had two bottles of type O blood. He's still giving him the second one."

They crowded into the tiny cabin next to the PA and the hooked stand that held a plastic bag of blood running down the tube into Arturo. Jamie had to stand next to Tom, touching him, very aware of his slightest move.

She didn't know if she wanted to say she was sorry or not.

Tom paid no attention to her. He chatted with the PA about how he had sewed up the wound, which had a large white bandage on it. Arturo lay unconscious.

"Do you think he will live?" Tom asked the PA.

He shrugged. "*No se.* I don't know. He'll probably lose his leg. He'll be weak for a long time. I told Jamie to keep giving him Mamacita's tea. It will help. I've done all I can do. Check with a doctor when you get to San Juan del Norte." The bag of blood was empty then, and the PA took his leave along with the stand.

Jamie stood at Tom's side staring at Arturo. "Is he still unconscious or is he just sleeping now?"

"I don't know. Either way, he'll be out for a while. Are you hungry? We passed that little café half-way up the road toward town. We can go get something to eat— together."

Her stomach growled at the thought of food. It didn't matter that Tom only wanted to make up for his anger. "Sure. I haven't eaten since this morning. The caiman got my lunch. Besides, it's dark out now and Julio's men won't look for us to arrive now."

At the café, Jamie avoided talking about how she

didn't like that he decided everything. Tom didn't bring it up either. *He doesn't care. Don't be stupid, of course he does.* She wrenched her attention back to what he was saying.

"...it's not taking as long to go down the river as I anticipated. Maybe on the way back we'll have time to tour the castle. The Spanish used it to keep the British from reaching Lake Nicaragua in the fifteen hundreds. Then, during the gold rush in California, ships carrying gold came down the Pacific coast to Nicaragua. Mule trains took the gold to Lake Nicaragua and ships loaded with it sailed down the San Juan, right past this castle, protected all the way to the Atlantic."

"You read this on my phone, right?"

"While we were on the ferry crossing the lake and you were talking to the packers."

"Yes, and now we're taking precious diamonds by the same route to the Atlantic to ship to New York."

"Right." Tom rubbed his chin. "Just think what it will do for this country if the Chinese really do build a canal across it. The shipping through the Panama Canal would shrink."

Tom chattered on about what it would do for the Nicaragua. Jamie imagined Mamacita enlarging her garden of medicinal plants and shipping them to Virginia, where Jamie's father's group would standardize them and package them into supplements to sell. All in all, the dinner relaxed her.

When they came back, stuffed with chorizo sausage, rice and beer, she was really sleepy. She'd slept only two or three hours last night. "Tom, are you tired too? You didn't get more than two hours last night."

"Yeah, really tired. You take the bunk, and I'll take a blanket out to the deck. My pack will make a good pillow. I'll cover with my slicker if it rains."

She slipped off her new clogs, fell into the bunk, and slept instantly. Two hours later she tossed and turned, in and out of dreams with machetes. *He's not cold on the deck, but he must be lonely.* She picked up her pillow and her blanket and went to the deck. He slept on his side on top of his folded blanket with his shirt off. The humidity kept the heat almost unbearable. She folded her blanket and laid it beside his. His back had dozens of mosquito bites. She went back to the cabin to fetch the cream Mamacita had given them. He woke as she rubbed it on his back. He rolled over and reached for her. She pushed his hand away and put cream on his face and hers. "Sleep," she told him. She lay down and rolled over to his back, spooned around him, and fell asleep.

In the morning, Jamie heard a voice calling from far away. She rolled off the blanket to the hard deck. *Ouch.*

Tom sat bolt upright, looking around wildly. He smiled when he caught her eye. "You slept with me. I like that."

Her face warmed. *I liked it too.*

He reached for her.

Arturo bellowed from the cabin. "Will you two lovebirds come in here and help me sit up? Can't you see that it's light already? We have to get going. I thought you wanted to get to San Juan del Norte today. Where's my bottle? Something to eat might be good too. And bring me a bucket to pee in."

Tom let go, laughing.

Jamie shook her head. "We're coming." She took the bucket into the cabin.

Tom raised Arturo's back and put the other pillow under him.

Arturo clung to his shirt and lectured him. "Lower. Put your arm lower. Pull me up higher so I can swing my legs to the floor. What's the matter? Why are you so slow? Why can't you help me with my legs? Ooh, be careful, that hurts."

"Hey, old man, I'll nursemaid you like Jamie if you don't be nice. She's tougher than I am."

Arturo looked shocked a moment. Then he chuckled. "You got me there, kid. Where's that pee bucket?"

Jamie handed him the bucket and set two of the extra sandwiches from the café on the counter. "I'm going to have my breakfast outside so you can have a minute of privacy. Be good, Arturo. We're so happy you're awake." She kissed him on the head, took a bottle of water and a sandwich, and walked back into the sunshine.

She sat on one of the crates and watched the water and the trees while she munched. A pair of howler monkeys called to each other across the river. A fish jumped and she felt the joy of living, a natural connection to the animals around her, and an excitement she thought came from surviving. She wondered how she could feel so content with Julio after them, the police up ahead, the argument with Tom, and the delivery man waiting for them.

What was his name? Guillermo Montoya. A guilty stab plagued her slightly when she thought that she had not even listed Uncle James. Well, they'd get to the jungle in time, she was sure.

She went back into the cabin. Tom was chatting with Arturo, his arm around him, steadying him in an upright position on the bed, with his feet on the floor. He kept his left leg with its white bandage, stretched out in front of him. "Let's get going. This is Monday," she announced. "We have to get to San Juan del Norte before six o'clock, because we promised Uncle James we would call while he has his satellite phone turned on. Are you ready to leave, old man?"

"Leave? You want to throw me out here in El Castillo? How do you think I'll get up the hill? No. You need me and my barge. You paid for me to take you to the port. Here I am. You need me to get you past the rapids and the police. Where's my bottle anyway?"

"You can have a swallow after you drink your tea. Then we'll leave for San Juan del Norte if you are up to it. Otherwise, why shouldn't we leave you here? That's what the agreement was." She was being harsh, but it was the only way to make him see the truth. He was too weak to help much. Tom put his hand on her hand on Arturo's knee though, frowning and shaking his head no behind Arturo's hanging head.

She waited while Arturo considered.

When he looked up, the old man studied her for a moment. "You don't fool me, Miss Jamie. You're not mean enough to leave me here. You fought to keep me alive, and I'll never forget it. The rapids are about five hundred feet after El Castillo. They will break up the barge and kill us if you hit the stones at the wrong angle. I will guide you through them and through the two other sets of rapids after that, if the two of you will help me up and out to sit on the bench beside your chair at the wheel. We can do it together."

Tom was nodding yes.

Arturo's stronger than I expected. "Okay. We'll try after your tea."

The old man groaned. "You never let a man win." But he was smiling.

After tea, and sips from his bottle, Jamie and Tom pulled him to a standing position. It was mostly Tom's strength that kept him moving as he fell forward out of the door to the bench in the wheelhouse. Tom sat beside him keeping him erect while he caught his breath.

"Well, what are we waiting for? Untie the boat, Miss Jamie."

Jamie wondered why she didn't mind his orders while she did mind Tom's. She untied the barge and slowly backed away from the wharf after Tom filled them up with gas from the pump on the dock.

"Keep the speed up, girl, so we have more turning control. In a few minutes, we'll have to make two tight turns. Keep in the middle of the river until I tell you."

She could hear a distant roar around the next bend. The river narrowed and ran faster. They passed the dock for the ferry and she saw it had departed, whether it was last night or this morning, she didn't know or care. She had to focus on the river.

"Left sharply to the middle of the river. Then an immediate ninety-degree right turn when I tell you and then a ninety-degree turn to the left when I tell you. You understand?"

Jamie nodded, worried she wouldn't hear him over the noise of the rushing water.

The sound increased. White splashes of foaming water hit a jumble of large rocks on the right side. The background roar blocked out her other thoughts. They headed straight for the rocks on the left bank of the river.

"Turn right *now*!" thundered over the roar. She jerked the wheel to the right, praying the long barge would not scrape the rocks on the left, and swing the bow into the huge boulder ahead on the left.

"Straighten the wheel," he called. "Immediate left."

Turn faster!

"Down the middle now."

The roar was lessening, and the rocks thinning.

"Keep watch. You'll see another big one right in the middle around the next bend. Circle it to the right and then straight ahead."

After the rock in the middle, only peaceful water confronted her. No white foam. Jamie slumped over the wheel and breathed deeply, trying to catch up on her oxygen. "We did it!"

The words slid out in triumph, but Arturo was already out, snoring, with his head on Tom's shoulder.

He shook Arturo. "Do you want to go lie on the bed again?"

Arturo pushed himself up and mumbled, "No. We are close to where the Rio San Juan is the border between Nicaragua and Costa Rica. The jungle will continue on the left side, broken only by two border guard stations on the left. The Costa Rican side of the river is not so high, and is often farmland cleared of trees." He rested a moment and then eyed Tom. "You don't want the police checking the barge, do you? They will check for goods smuggled out of Costa Rica. They might want to see in the crates, depending on their mood. You might have to bribe them."

"We don't have enough to bribe them. They would expect thousands of córdobas."

"Yes, so we'll throw out the anchor when we get near the border in about a half hour, and we will wait. Every day at ten and at two, the guards patrol the border between their station and up river to where the border of Costa Rica begins. We will stop two turns before the border and wait for an hour or so, depending on the time."

It sounded good to Jamie, but what about the time? "I hope it won't make us late. We have to get to the Atlantic by six."

"Don't worry, little lady. You already got us through the worst of the obstacles. We'll be in San Juan del Norte by four or five."

"Lean on my shoulder until we anchor, old man. While we wait, I'll hammer those boxes tight with the nails I bought, so the border guards can't open them, if they do stop us."

Arturo's snoring began in less than a minute.

Jamie's spirits were high. "Tom," she whispered as they glided quietly and steadily down the middle of the river. "When we're on the way back, we'll be stopping at El Castillo again, won't we?"

Arturo's eyes opened, but Tom couldn't see. "And?"

"Yes, tell us," Arturo said with a grin.

Tom pushed him aside. "Don't butt in."

Jamie sighed. No use being shy around Arturo. "With the boxes gone, Julio won't be a problem. We can have a fancy meal and spend the night at the hotel instead of on the boat." She knew what Tom wanted.

"It's a date," he answered. "Be quiet, old man."

"I'm not so old," Arturo mumbled. "I spent a night in the hotel with Mamacita once." His head drooped onto Tom's shoulder again.

Chuckling inside, Jamie turned back to the wheel.

The next couple of hours passed swiftly. They waited for the border guards to do their patrol. Tom nailed the crates. They went through another set of rapids. Jamie just had to keep to the right.

At the next border guard station a loudspeaker hailed them. "Hello, Captain Arturo. What do you have on the barge today?"

"Don't worry," Arturo told Tom. "The lieutenant knows me. I did him a favor once. Stand up and tell him 'car parts.'"

Tom hollered, and the loudspeaker answered, "Pass."

Arturo looked rather tired. "Only one more set of rapids, about an hour from San Juan del Norte. Keep to the left, but not too far to the left. Put the engine in neutral for now, Jamie. Maybe you two can help me lie down in the bunk right now, so I can sleep a bit?"

He's going to be all right, she thought, *if only he doesn't lose his leg.*

With Tom at the wheel, Jamie got another cup of tea into the old man before he fell asleep.

ᏋᏝᏋᏝ

Tom reveled in the quiet that followed. Only one small set of rapids to navigate, and they'd reach their destination, San Juan del Norte. *We'll look for Montoya's warehouse right away. I hope Julio's gang doesn't show up.* The memory of chopping off that guy's hand brought back the sick feeling and Julio's voice yelling "murderer." Tom didn't want to kill anybody, but he would fight if he had to.

Jamie came out of the cabin and handed him a sandwich. "I'm getting tired of sandwiches. Aren't you?" She glanced up. "The sky is getting really dark. I hope it doesn't storm before we go through the last rapids."

"Don't worry. It's only two o'clock. One way or another we'll be at the warehouse in two hours with plenty of time to hand over the crates, find an internet café, call the FBI, and talk to Uncle James at six o'clock. Piece of cake. This ham sandwich is pretty good when you're hungry." *I won't remind her that Julio might find us.* The sick feeling took hold of him again. "Jamie, I want to ask you something. Don't laugh—it's not about making love this time. You remember I chopped off the hand of one of Julio's men Saturday night during the fight?"

She nodded. "Yes?"

"Well, I wondered…you care so much about people's lives, yet you've never said peep about me being a killer. I feel awful about it. Julio called me a murderer. I think I am." He ran his hand through his hair. "Here, take the wheel. I have to walk."

"Okay. Walk, but keep talking."

"I know I had to do it to save *our* lives, and I hope the police never find out. Still, what do *you* think about me? Remember the statues in Granada? I keep thinking about the jaguar on the head of that one chief. I feel the jaguar in me. Am I some sort of animal acting out of gut instinct?" He swung around to look at her, intent on her answer.

"Oh, Tom, we all have animal parts to us that take over in times of danger. Instincts are good that way. You saved us. At the same time, you are the sweetest, kindest, gentlest person I have ever known. It's the civilized part of you that I respect, but it's the way you saved our lives that makes me love you." She chuckled. "That sounds so hi-falutin', but it's true."

His shoulders slumped in relief. His arms went around her from behind, and he kissed her head. "I was afraid I might lose you."

She pulled away enough to look up at him, her eyes crinkled. "Tom," she questioned, "what did you think of me? I didn't hesitate to swing that machete at those pirates."

He rubbed her cheek with his thumb. "Don't worry, kitten. We were both desperate to stay alive, and to keep those cases we have to deliver in order to fetch your uncle. You're all about saving lives—your own, mine, Uncle James's, and Arturo's. I'll always love that about you." He squeezed her. He enjoyed the way she rubbed his chest before she turned away.

It began to rain, and in moments buckets came down. The canvas overhead thundered. It felt good wrapped around Jamie while Mother Nature pounded them. They huddled under the canvas. Lightning bolts crossed the sky, one deafening rumble after another.

Something flew over his head and Jamie's. A rope! It tightened and he struggled to turn. Jamie screamed.

"We got you," Julio's voice cried out. "Hah! You didn't hear us board because of the rain."

The thunder almost drowned out Tom's swearing. "You son of a bitch. There's no fucking way you'll get away with this."

"You tell him, Tom," Jamie cried.

Two men grabbed Tom's arms and Julio pulled the rope off, taking hold of Jamie when she pounded on him.

"Throw him overboard," Julio ordered.

"No! No!" he heard Jamie scream as the two men dragged him through the cabin.

Arturo had pushed himself up and reached out to grab the pants leg of the man on Tom's left. It was just enough to catch the man's attention. Tom slipped one arm out of the man's grasp. He fell into the other man, jabbing him with his elbow. He jerked free and ran into the pouring rain on the deck. He reached for the case that held the machetes, but as he leaned over, the two men grasped him again and lifted him over the rail. He tumbled through the air, and the water closed over his head before he could breathe in.

Chapter 9

The Jungle and the Escape

Jamie pried at Julio's fingers. She had to get loose to run to Tom. "Don't throw him overboard, you idiots. You need him." Julio didn't listen.

"Put the boat in reverse. I want you to watch him drown."

Jamie choked. He was damn evil. She put the engine in reverse, and Julio dragged her into the storm at the port rail. The boat slowed and the water began passing them, swirling in the wind accompanying the storm and the backwash of the reversing engine. She clung to the rail, her tears mingling with the heavy drops pounding her head, running down her face. *He can't have drowned yet. Where is he? Where is he?*

Far ahead of the boat now, an arm shot out of the water and Tom's head popped up. "Swim, Tom, swim," she whispered into the rain, her hands clutching the rail, trying to help him. He disappeared around the next bend to the left.

Jamie fought Julio, struggling to get out of his grip. He slowly pulled her back to the wheel.

"Steer the boat again before we hit that bank, you crazy woman."

"No. You can have the diamonds. I don't care if the boat sinks," she sobbed. "I want Tom."

Arturo still leaned on the door of the cabin. He shook his head. "Take the wheel, Jamie."

The barge swung toward the southern bank as the river curved left. Jamie steered the boat hard to the left. The river, widened by all the tributary streams and rivers behind them, was narrowing again. The flood of water rushed through the narrowing gap.

"Rapids," Arturo called weakly, and slumped to the floor in the doorway.

Jamie heard him. *Keep to the left, but not too far.* As the barge came around the bend, both the current and the motor were taking them. She kept to the left, avoiding the big rock. Her eyes swung from the foamy water off the starboard to the narrow path down the middle to the rock on the left. She saw movement against the rock. Two arms and a head clung to it. Tom. Her heart surged. She swung her arm to the right, pointing to the foam washing against the rocks. "Julio, tell me if we get too close to the rocks. Watch for small ones."

Julio kept his eyes to the right and didn't see Tom as they swept by.

Dear God, take care of my Tom. The river widened and calmed somewhat despite the storm, which seemed to be lessening a bit. *Tom is strong. He'll get to the bank. It's only a couple of meters to the bank. No caimans here. The current's too swift.*

Five minutes later, Julio pushed her aside. "Go into the cabin. I'll handle the wheel. I just needed you for the rapids." He called for his men to get the old man Arturo out of the way.

Jamie got her arm under the old man on one side and the man called Juan took the other and they lifted. Arturo was a dead weight. Nevertheless, he managed to complain to Juan.

"Owww! You're hurting me. Don't twist me. What's the matter with you? Can't you see I'm sick? Don't let go. I'll fall. I can't make it. Are you the one that did this to me?"

Juan shoved him toward the bunk. "Shut up, old man."

"Owww! Leave me alone. Let this woman check my bandage. I think I'm bleeding again. I'll probably die." He turned his head and winked at Jamie. "Don't let me drop onto the bunk. I'll hit my head, you horse's ass."

Juan dumped him on the bed.

"Owww! Now fetch me the bucket from the deck to pee in before it's too late."

Jamie pulled the chest from under the bunk and sat beside him. She checked his bandage. No sign of bleeding.

When Juan came back with the bucket, Arturo hollered, "You get out of here now and give a man some privacy. This woman will take care of me."

Juan grumbled and left to join the other two men on the deck. They checked the crates and chattered about diamonds. A light mist was all that remained of the storm.

Jamie was sure they didn't know about the military arsenal inside.

"Arturo, Tom is alive." She hugged him. "He clung onto that big rock on the left. I saw him. He'll probably make it the couple of meters to the shore." She glanced out the small cabin window. "Look at all that jungle." Her voice rose and wavered. "How will he make it to civilization? He has nothing. What can we do?" She snuffled again.

Arturo took her hand. "Hush, little lady. Tom is good at taking care of himself. Besides, villages and farms line the banks between here and the town. Now listen. I have an idea."

"Will it save Tom?"

"No. He'll have to do that himself. But it might save you and your Uncle James."

She couldn't smile about that. She patted his cheek. "Okay, I'll listen."

Arturo pushed himself up on his elbow. "I'm a lot better than they think. I'm going to pretend I'm too weak to tell them where to go when we get into the river estuary. The river actually goes straight out to the ocean, but San Juan del Norte is up the Rio Indio where it enters the San Juan on the left. You'll have to tell that rat Julio that you think the town is straight ahead, and he'll be out in the ocean before he knows it, and he'll have to turn back. Meantime, I'll figure a way to get my machete from the deck.

"It will be up to you to convince Julio to take the diamonds to San Juan del Norte, and not take them back to San Carlos. When we get to town we'll use the machete to escape and get to the warehouse before they do, and then we'll persuade that man…Montoya, is it?…to help us get rid of Julio and take possession of the diamond crates. I know it's a little far-fetched, but it might work."

She stared at him. "That will never work. You're still too weak. Even if you get the machete, you can't handle it."

"Trust me, little lady. I can be stronger if I try. Besides, you can handle a machete. I saw you."

Jamie shuddered. "You didn't see me afterward. It was so horrible. I vomited over the rail." She hesitated. "I admit, Arturo, I can't think of anything better. We'll have to try your plan."

ჟიჟ

When his head popped out of the water Tom sucked in air and choked on the rain water that filled it. Spluttering, he looked around and automatically stroked. He couldn't see anything, no barge, no jungle shore, just dark gray. The current pulled him down the center of the river. He turned ninety degrees to the left to swim to the shore, but the current that swept him down the river was stronger than his strokes. He saw the bank ahead of him, but couldn't get any closer. Suddenly the river curved and the current pulled him to the left. His foot hit a rock but it didn't slow him.

I'm strong. He stroked harder for the green mass in front of him. His left arm slammed into a large rock. He tried to grab onto it despite the pain, and his right arm slid along the rock and finally gripped on an outcropping. He pulled his left arm in against the current and found another handhold. He rested several minutes, his head barely out of the water. He heard the roar of water hitting rocks and remembered the rapids they had been approaching. He didn't dare look. If he lost his grip the deadly current would sweep him into the rocks. From the corner of his eyes he saw the barge slip past, not ten feet from him.

Handhold by handhold he pulled himself around to the leeside of the rock, ignoring the shooting pains in his left wrist. The current slowed here and he stroked more surely to the green wall. The river channel cut deep here, and the cliff, covered with vines and bushes leaning over the water, stretched steeply to thirty feet above him. He grabbed the first branch he could reach and heaved himself closer until his feet touched ground on the six-inch wide beach.

The rain was lessening. He could see the rapids across the river. The barge was lost to sight.

The only way out is up. Ugh. He studied the vines. He tugged on the root of the biggest. It didn't budge, so he pulled himself up with his right arm on the heaviest branch he could find, put his left foot on the vine root and pushed up. He steadied himself with his aching wrist a moment, and then reached with his right arm and did it again.

Step by step. Just like my whole life. I can do it. When he reached the top a half hour later; he found the edge of the cliff covered thickly with tree trunks and underbrush reaching for the light. He moved through the dripping undergrowth. The sun came out and he and the bushes steamed. About twenty feet away from the cliff edge the brush thinned. Much less greenery blocked his way here in the dim light under the canopy and fewer mosquitoes bit. Probably fewer snakes too.

Jamie, don't let that man hurt you. Stay alive for me. Julio will probably go to the warehouse in town. I have no choice.

If he walked under the canopy parallel to the river he'd eventually come to something.

芭ϡ芭ϡ

Jamie gave the last sandwich to Arturo. "You need the strength," was her easy excuse. She couldn't possibly eat now. Her stomach lurched every time she thought about what they were going to try to do. That was the whole reason she felt uneasy. They would try, but they wouldn't succeed.

"Arturo, listen. I need Tom. These last three days have made me realize how much I need him. I always thought I could take care of myself, but he has taken care of me since Uncle James called. I don't think I can go on without him. I'm too scared." She wanted to hear something encouraging.

Arturo frowned. "Jamie, I may have exaggerated a few minutes ago about how much I can do. The truth is I'm counting on you to do most of it. Don't quit now. Remember when you told me to hold the tourniquet myself or else I would die? You have to take care of yourself now. You don't want to die at the hand of that cruel man."

Julio called then, and Jamie rose, her legs reluctant to move toward him. If he threw her overboard, thinking he didn't need her, what would she do? She'd have to swim. The current wasn't so bad now. Maybe she could steal the motorboat that they pulled behind them. The fear of death can make all sorts of possibilities run through your mind, she thought.

Julio told her to sit on the bench. "See this?" He pointed to the bandage on his calf. "Seven stitches. Look at my face." He pointed to the purple bruise on his temple and his black eye. "Tell me some answers or you'll feel my revenge."

"What do you want to know?" She leaned forward, arms on her knees, studying the floor. She couldn't stand to look at him.

"Where are you supposed to deliver these diamonds?"

She straightened. He didn't know what he was going to do with them. "To Guillermo Montoya's warehouse. Do you know where it is?"

"You'll take me to him. That useless bargeman won't be any help."

Jamie's mind sorted out the steps of Arturo's plan. "I can take you to the town. The river splits up so much here in the delta, but I think I can find the main stream to the ocean. You'll have to let me keep Arturo alive so he can tell me what I need to know. If I help you get to the warehouse dock, you'll have to let us go. If you do, I won't go to the police, because I'd be in trouble too." She got up to stand beside him, her shoulders tight across her back, while he thought about her proposal, "What are you going to do with the diamonds? You can't take them to New York or Amsterdam, where they have diamond cutters to process the raw diamonds. If you know how much the diamonds are actually worth, you can probably negotiate with Montoya, and demand a ransom for half of what they will bring."

A frown etched Julio's face. Clearly he had no idea what to do with the raw diamonds now that he had them. Maybe this was the first time he thought about it. He ran his hand through his hair.

If he doesn't agree with me, he'll have to kill us before we get to the warehouse.

"You help me with Montoya and I'll let you go."

"And Arturo also."

"Sure. Why would I want him? Once I have the money from the diamonds, I'll just go back to San Carlos, or anywhere I please. Maybe I'll keep a couple of diamonds for myself."

Jamie backed into the cabin, watching Julio spend

money in his head. "So far, so good," she whispered to Arturo.

Arturo stroked his chin in thought. "Now we have to get the three men off the back deck to the wheelhouse, so we can get the machetes."

She nodded. They passed several tributaries in the next half hour, each widening the river. The jungle disappeared now and small trees and bushes covered the north side on flat land. The number of sand bars increased. They passed the Rio Indio, the tributary where San Juan was located.

She made Julio and Juan carry the reluctant Arturo to the bench by the wheel, saying he needed to tell Julio how to avoid the sand bars, because they shifted in the delta every year. It was true.

Julio couldn't stand the constant screeching and complaining. He called Juan and they carried Arturo back to the bunk. "Shut up, old man, or I'll throw you in the water too."

Arturo huddled helplessly, as if terrified.

When they passed the last island and the ocean was straight ahead, she told Julio, "You take the wheel out into the Atlantic and turn north. I think the town of San Juan is ten miles north in a small bay. The warehouse is the first dock inside the bay. Arturo's asleep. I need to wake him and give him some tea."

In the cabin Arturo sat up, his feet on the floor. "Now?" he asked.

"No, not now. I've got this." She pushed the grumbling man back onto the bed. "Shhhh."

She walked onto the deck where Julio's three men leaned on the rail, enjoying the rising ocean breeze drying them off. All three wore machetes in their belts. She swallowed. It was hard, but she walked up to them anyway ratcheting up her confidence.

She leaned on the rail with them, taking a good look at the boat tied to the stern. "Is that the boat you arrived in? It's just a skiff."

Juan answered expansively, "Si. The motor is big, and powerful enough to catch you. We spotted you going through the rapids at El Castillo this morning."

Just to impress him that he didn't frighten her, she spit out a few of her favorite swear words. The three men looked at her as if she were an anaconda.

Juan grinned. "We have the diamonds now. You didn't even hear us because of the storm. It was so easy."

She heaved a big sigh to let them know they had won.

"You were just lucky." She paused. "Have any of you ever seen the ocean before?" she asked, not looking them in the eye.

The three hesitated. "No, none of us have. Are we close?"

"Yes. The ocean will amaze you. It's so big, and the breeze is so cool. The beach sand is so white. Gulls fly overhead, screeching. Everything smells like salt. The water we're in right now is salty, not fresh like in the San Carlos bay. Every time I come to the ocean I get this feeling of freedom, like the whole world is waiting for me." The men's mouths opened slightly, their eyes wide.

"Julio said you could come to the wheelhouse and see the ocean with him. You won't be afraid of the big waves, will you?"

Juan eyed the other two. "Uh, no. We aren't little kids." All three hurried through the cabin past an open-mouthed Arturo.

Jamie gestured to Arturo to stay on the bed. She opened the case and took out the two machetes, careful not to cut herself with the sharp edges. She rushed back to the cabin and put them gently under the mattress of her bunk. She sat on top of them, pleased with her accomplishment. "Would you like some tea, Arturo?"

He chuckled. "Certainly, señorita."

ↄ৩ৎↄ

Tom pushed on. He watched for any sign of civilization—a clearing in the jungle, a road, a village. He could stand at the cliff's edge and watch for kayakers who would tell him where the nearest village was, but that would take hours. Both Jamie and his father, the people he cared about, were far away. He was alone. Besides, every time he brushed into one of the bushes clouds of mosquitoes rose. The cream Jamie had put on him last night was long gone. He groaned. *I have to get to Jamie.* Who knew what Julio would do to her?

No breeze penetrated the jungle. The heat and humidity cooked him. His clothes were still sopping wet. He studied the vines climbing the trees here under the canopy. Some were a foot thick at their base. One particular species of tree rose far above the general height of the other trees—the ceiba. Maybe he could climb one and spot the nearest village.

He tugged on the vine climbing one of the tall trees and it didn't move. In the dim light he tried to make out how high the vine grew. Something moved way up there. A ten-foot mottled gray snake was slithering down the trunk toward him. A boa constrictor? It made him angry. He was so tired and miserable he wanted to fight back, but all he had was the knife in his pocket. He backed away from the tree and marched on with long steps.

He heard a dog bark and froze. Another bark. He began to run as best he could between the trees, slipping on the wet rotting jungle floor until he came to a row of logs leading toward the cliff edge with a cleared path on the other side of it. Steps led down about ten feet to the dock on the river. He hadn't noticed he'd been going downhill.

Tom ran, shouting, up the path, burst out of the trees into a small clearing with a cement block house. Beyond it lay a cleared field, filled with planted corn. The dog was chasing a small deer from the field. Civilization. In the shade of the jungle trees stood an old muddy pick-up. The truck might save him.

Now he could get to Jamie. He headed toward the back door, calling hello.

A small boy came out of the door and called to the open doorway, "Mama, a man came out of the jungle."

A pregnant woman with a machete in her hand appeared and pushed the child inside. She looked at Tom's filthy tee shirt and shorts. "You're a tourist. Did you fall out of your kayak?"

Tom stood back out of reach of her machete and explained that men had pirated the barge he was on and had thrown him overboard. He left out the diamonds and the military hardware. "Can your husband take me to San Juan del Norte in the truck so I can tell the police?"

The woman let the machete fall. "San Juan has one policeman for the whole town. Can you pay us for the gas?"

Tom took his soaking wet wallet from his pocket. Glued together by the water, the Nicaraguan bills were wet enough to separate. He began peeling off the córdobas and then just handed her the whole wad. "It's just a little less than a thousand. You can have the whole bunch if you'll take me right now."

She took the money immediately. "Thank you. That is a lot of money. My husband is working in a field down by the road. I'll take you to him."

Five minutes later, Tom waited in the truck with the little boy while she explained to the short man who was her husband. She showed him the bunch of córdobas. He handed her the hoe.

When he climbed in he introduced himself. "Me llamo Tomàs." He put out his hand.

Tom laughed, feeling better, excited that they were moving. "My name is Tom too. My girlfriend is on the barge also. I don't know what the pirates might do to her. Can we hurry?" He glanced at his watch. Thank god it was waterproof. "It was about two thirty when they threw me in the water. Can you take me to the warehouse on the beach? That's where the barge is going."

"What time is it now?" Tomàs asked. He didn't have a watch.

"Four o'clock. How long will it take to get to town?"

"Not too long."

Only a half hour. The little boy stared at him the whole while. He reached up once and brushed Tom's cheek with his hand. "Your face is dirty."

He must not be used to seeing many people. Tom couldn't pay attention to him, though. All he could think about was Jamie. What if he got to the barge too late? He would search for her at the nearest internet café. Julio probably won't kill her without a reason. *Of course, she does have a temper. She might be dead.* He felt strangled. "Hurry, *por favor.*"

They drove through town, passing a couple of hotels and eating places, but no visible internet café on the main street. Tomàs said the eco-hotel beyond the warehouse had one. At the far end of town, Tomàs pulled up at a large building of cement block, and Tom got out. An empty dock stretched ten meters out into the bay. Beyond the dock a large boathouse rose. His chest tightened. Jamie. After five o'clock and no barge. *Is that good or bad? Where is she?*

He pounded on the windowless office door.

❧❦❧

Jamie watched Julio's back. He was loud and boisterous and his three fellow thieves clapped him on the back and shouted great hurrahs into the ocean breeze. She really did hate him. Julio began the turn north.

"Arturo, now is the time, but we aren't going to attack them with the machetes. Two against four is not very good odds for us. While they're not looking we'll get into the boat we're pulling. If it doesn't take us too long to start the motor, we'll be away before they know it."

"No, I can't do it."

Jamie's breath caught. "I can't leave you behind."

"You must. They won't kill me. They will need me in a minute when they can't find the town. I'll distract them while you get in the boat. You need to get to Montoya first. He'll help you get the diamonds and help you find Tom. Now go."

"But…" It was hard to accept, no matter how right he was.

"Go. Take both machetes. I'll see you again."

She took a long look at him and kissed him on the forehead. After glancing at Julio and his men, she picked up her pack and Tom's, the two machetes, and the gym bag. She crossed to the stern deck and tossed the packs into the boat when she heard Arturo screaming at Julio for coming too close to the Atlantic shore. He continued hollering for some time. When Julio told his men to take him to his bunk, Arturo shrieked even louder, and Jamie threw the machetes in the boat, praying that the men didn't hear the clang. She jumped in after them and pulled the cord on the motor. It didn't catch until the second pull. Julio was shouting. Using the machete, she chopped through the rope tying the boat and looked up.

Julio's eyes burned at her. "I'll catch you in San Juan, you little liar. You'll be sorry when I cut your tongue out."

She swung the boat wide and turned back toward the Rio Indio.

Chapter 10

Smugglers vs. Pirates

The door opened and a burly man confronted Tom. His fat cheeks and cleft chin seemed familiar. Someone in Managua? Not important now.

"Are you Guillermo Montoya?"

"No. He's in the warehouse. We're expecting a shipment so make it fast." He waved Tom in through the door and through the office inside, on into the warehouse.

The one large room had rows of pallets stacked with crates. Tom sucked in his breath.

Montoya will be a dangerous man. He's the smuggler. Esposito and Estrella just handle arrangements from their offices. I'll have to make him think I'm dangerous, if I want to convince him we can get Jamie and the cargo back.

Tom scrutinized the room. Two men in the back corner were talking. The tall man with the soft voice wore a gun belt. He had to be the boss.

Strength. I have to show strength. Adrenalin energy poured through him. *The power of the jaguar…*

He marched over to the man with the gun. "Montoya?"

"Yes? Who are you?"

"Come with me to your office. I have information to tell you."

Montoya frowned and glanced at the man who had escorted Tom in. The man shrugged his shoulders.

Tom boldly walked to the office. Montoya followed. *So far, so good.*

When Montoya closed the door of the small room that held one old desk, Tom turned on him immediately. "Who's in charge, you or Estrella?" He doubted it was Espinosa. He was just the clerk who gave them the job.

Montoya rested his hand on his gun. His soft voice lowered. "Who do you think you are? What business is this of yours?"

"I know who has the diamonds and the guns."

Montoya leaned over Tom, grabbed his shirt front, and pulled a gun, shoving it into Tom's stomach. "I said who are you?"

Tom didn't flinch. He couldn't back down now. On the other hand, he didn't want Montoya to shoot him. He put his hands up. "Whoa. I'm Tom Kirk, and I'm trying to help you."

"How do you know what I do?" Montoya demanded, his voice intense and softer yet.

"Estrella hired my partner and me to bring your crates from San Carlos, but a small gang of thieves knew we had diamond cores and attacked us. They threw me overboard. I walked through the jungle to get here."

Montoya shoved him back, taking the pistol from his stomach.

Thank God.

"How do you know about the guns, and why do you want to help me?"

Tom's heartbeat slowed a bit. Montoya was listening. Tom deliberately turned his back to him to show he wasn't afraid. He didn't think the man would shoot him until he got answers. He played with a pen on the desk. "When we went through the rapids at El Castillo, one crate overturned, hit the deck on the corner, and broke open. I was worried it was drugs, so I opened one of the cylinders. When I saw the machine guns, I opened one of the big crates and found the rocket launchers." He turned back to see if Montoya might shoot him for knowing about the military hardware.

Montoya waved the gun at him. "Go on. The river pirates took the barge? Where are they now?"

"They're coming here. The leader of the gang, Julio Juarez, doesn't know about the guns and rocket launchers. He will want to sell the raw diamonds to you for cash."

"Why don't I just shoot you and shoot the thieves when they get here?" Montoya speculated. "They don't have any guns, do they?"

"You are right about that, Guillermo." Tom called

him by the first name to prove they were equals. "However, if you shoot me, the whole United States Government will come down on you when they start searching for me, and that would be the end of your smuggling. On the other hand, if you don't shoot me, I can't tell on you because the Nicaraguan Government would put me in jail, along with you, for delivering the guns." He tapped the pen on the desk, whirled, and stepped up close to Montoya, forcing him to step back. "Who's in charge, you or Estrella?" he snapped, callous to the danger now.

Montoya stiffened and snarled a threat in his soft voice. "Why do you want to know? It doesn't matter."

"I think Estrella is making more money than you, and you are the one taking the risk. Maybe Estrella might have set those thieves on you to take the diamonds and guns back. Just think, he could send them north on a drone. He doesn't need you." Tom pointed the pen at Montoya. "And you don't need him. Once you get the shipment, you can send them to your buyer in New York and keep all the cash for yourself."

He walked forward a step driving Montoya to the wall. The tall man slumped for a moment and then looked straight at him.

Uh oh. Maybe I pushed him too far. I want him to trust me enough to let me help him get the crates and take care of Julio. He has a gun, and Julio doesn't. If I get on the boat, I can get Jamie away from that SOB and then we can get the paperwork and head back to Managua for the cash.

Montoya had a strange look on his face. It was more

thoughtful than angry. "I don't need Estrella. He can find someone else to smuggle for him." His eyes flashed and he grinned at Tom. "You hear that? I don't need Estrella. That Chinese man who is in town to begin the dredging for the new canal across Nicaragua to the Pacific will make this a big port. He'll be importing and exporting all kinds of things, and he'll want to hire my submarine."

Submarine? That's how the weapons are going to New York. It must be in the boathouse.

Montoya's eyes narrowed. "I won't let Estrella cheat me. I want that military hardware back. That cell in New York is paying plenty."

Cell? Maybe Montoya will tell me who it is that is getting the weapons. I can tell the FBI. "Cell?"

"Si. The terrorist cell in New York City will pay me a million for these weapons." Montoya surged from the wall, and the pistol was in Tom's stomach again. "You want to help me? Why?"

"My fiancée is on the barge. I want her back. I want you to get the crates and give me the paperwork so I can take it to Estrella and get paid for the delivery. I don't want him to cheat *me* either."

Montoya rubbed his chin, his eyes hard. The gun muzzle jabbed deeper into Tom's belly. "How do you propose to help me?" he asked in the controlled soft voice again.

I won't back down now. My jaguar heart is stirring. Julio will be his prey.

"When the barge docks here, Julio will want to negotiate. Tell him you'll trade me for my fiancée, and then you'll talk. Tell him you want to get rid of me, but you can use the girl for ransom. He'll like the idea of having another chance to murder me. Put your gun in my belt in the middle of my back and tie my hands loosely behind. Julio will take the bait and you will pass me to the barge after my Jamie is on the dock. I'll take the gun out and shoot Julio. Then you and your two men can board, and we'll take Julio's three, and you'll get the crates. You only have one policeman in town. He'll believe us when we explain they are thieves." He stopped talking.

"You mean this gun?" Montoya gave Tom another painful jab. "I don't give this gun to anybody."

Part of Tom was relieved. The jaguar persisted. "Guillermo, I won't—"

Someone knocked on the warehouse door. "Boss, a boat is coming."

Montoya and Tom ran through the warehouse and out to the beach. It wasn't the barge. Tom saw the tiny figure in a skiff and exploded toward the end of the dock. Jamie had escaped Julio somehow. He saw the big grin and heard her whooping and calling.

He reached for her and pulled her to the dock and into his arms. The warmth of her clinging body grew to a promise.

≈≈≈

Jamie rained kisses on Tom, and found herself erupting in tears. "Tom, I was so scared. What if I never found you?" She leaned back a little, looking him in the face, and wiped her tears. She brushed a leaf from his brown hair and wiped a dirt smudge from his cheek. "You are so filthy." A smile tugged a corner of her mouth up. "But you're really here. You have to tell me what you've been through." With her arms shaking, she pulled him close again and hugged him tight, knowing she'd never get enough of him. For a long moment, Tom's arms comforted her, calmed her.

Tom pulled back a little and ran his hands through her hair. "Tell me about Julio and the diamonds. Are they coming or did you whack them all with the machetes, you and Arturo?"

She chuckled and reached down to grab the drifting skiff to tie it. "No, I didn't. In fact, Julio will be here with Arturo and the barge any minute. He intends for Montoya to pay him a big ransom for the diamonds."

Tom's eyes turned down river. "I don't see him yet. Don't worry. Montoya and I have a plan."

She examined the tall thin man who was watching her. Two men with machetes stood behind him. "Good." She reached down to the boat again. "Here's your pack and your machete and here's Arturo's for me."

"For you? Oh no. I just got you back. You wait in the warehouse. Montoya and I will take care of Julio."

Jamie's hand fell from his arm, her face warming. She loved the man, but he sure did like to tell her what to do. "That man Montoya is going to help? Yes. It makes sense." She looked Montoya over, trying to figure what kind of man he was. Pretty dangerous, judging from the outraged look on his face. His hand rested on a pistol. That was bad. He might kill somebody without a thought.

He inched toward her, but Tom stepped between and put his hand on Montoya's chest to stop him. That surprised her. Tom wasn't afraid of him.

"Listen, Jamie. Four of us against four of them, and we have a gun. You can be safe. Montoya will tell Julio he wants you for ransom. If you want, we'll tie you up and leave you outside the warehouse door so you can watch."

"Like a dog? I'm not your chattel." She was steaming now, breathing deeply. "I am as much responsible for these diamonds being delivered as you." She glanced at Montoya, who was watching her intently. *Does he know that we know about the guns?* Montoya stepped even closer and she stepped back in alarm. *He thinks I'm "just a woman."* She stepped forward again. Montoya didn't budge. "You men can't treat me like this. I'm not a plaything," she said, full into Montoya's face. She felt a little guilty, using the fact that she was a woman. They wouldn't hurt her.

"We will do with you what we wish," Montoya said, his teeth bared. "First, we will lure the bastard thieves onto the beach, promising to negotiate. Then we'll kill them and get our goods. It's a good plan." He shrugged.

She opened her mouth to retort, but said nothing because a small stocky man was approaching, holding the hand of a little boy. The men turned.

"Tomàs, what are you doing here?" Tom asked.

Tomàs stood, feet apart in a sturdy stance. "I want my boy to see that sometimes men need to fight for what is theirs."

Jamie and everyone else, including Montoya's two men, took a deep breath.

"Okay," Montoya said.

"I will go get the policeman while you get the pirates off the boat. You have a plan for that, right?"

"Yes, of course," Montoya replied.

"You will not need to kill anyone. I don't want my son to see that. You can just tie them up and we'll take them to jail."

No killing. You hear that? That's what I was going to say. Jamie shot a triumphant look at Tom and Montoya. "Yes, we don't have to kill anyone. As much as I hate Julio, I'd rather keep him alive to go to court."

Tomàs nodded at her.

Maybe he thought she was the boss. Fat chance of that in this country.

"I see a barge coming. I'll go get the policeman now." He left with his little boy, and she swung around to look for the barge.

"How are we going to get them off the barge to negotiate?" she asked. "If Julio sees you, Tom, he won't come ashore."

Tom looked a bit uneasy.

"Tell me."

"Well, they won't see the gun…"

"You'll have a *gun*?" Somehow it shocked her that Tom might actually use a gun, despite his dislike of them. She glanced at his dirt-covered scar.

Tom stared right at her. He looked so…decided. "The plan is to tie me up loosely with my hands behind me, and Montoya's gun tucked into my belt at the back," he explained in a steady voice. "I will be the bait. Montoya will offer me to Julio. Julio will take the bait because he wants me dead, so he will have complete control of the diamonds. He will think he and his three men versus Montoya and his two will be good odds. Furthermore, he has possession of the diamonds."

She grabbed his arm instinctively. "So you're going to take the gun out and shoot Julio? You really think you want to do that?"

"That was the plan when I thought I had to get you off the ship and away from Julio."

"Well, you don't have to do it now to rescue me, but Arturo still has to be rescued. We can't let Julio hurt him. It's Arturo's boat, and we need it to get back to Managua as fast as possible." She hesitated, eyes down, working up the courage to say what she really was thinking. "You and Captain Ricardo saved our lives from Julio. It was Julio's fault that you had to defend us by stopping that man from boarding the boat. You don't have to prove you're brave to me, or to yourself. You don't have to shoot anyone."

"Women," Montoya mumbled under his breath.

Jamie hardened her mind against him and listened to the silence that followed. Tom flicked the machete she had handed him against his knee, looking down the river at the barge in the distance.

Montoya took Tom's arm and then dropped it. "Ten minutes. I want my diamonds. We have to prepare. I'll even let you use my gun. Help me, Tom, and I'll sign those papers for you to take to Estrella. After he pays you, tell him he and I are through."

Jamie watched Tom, while the machete flicked. When he turned to her, he had that look again, his lips thin and determined.

"Jamie, let them tie you up by the warehouse door with only a loop around your hands so you can get loose. We'll take Julio and his men, and then you board the barge and help Arturo. We have to settle this quickly. Remember, we have to call Uncle James by six-thirty, and it's six now. I'll just shoot the gun in the air to scare them."

Montoya clapped him on the shoulder and sent his two men for ropes. They tied her with a loop around her hands and then tied it to the doorknob.

She mused on it. *I can put on a good show here, pretending I can't get loose. Mmm. Thirty feet of beach to cross to get to the dock.*

Montoya's men put several loops around Tom's arms and shoulders as well as tying his hands behind. Montoya took his gun belt off, weighed his pistol in his hands before stuffing it in Tom's shorts where Julio couldn't see it. Montoya took Tom's machete. Julie grimaced. *Too bad. It looks so natural on Tom.* Montoya's men took hold of Tom on each side and their boss stood in front of them, hiding Tom. They waited.

The barge came within hailing distance, Julio at the wheel. "I see you are waiting for us," he called. "Get some cash ready. A lot of it."

Montoya sent a man back to the warehouse. He

rushed past Jamie, and came out a few moments later with a large bundle of córdobas that he took to Montoya. The barge slowly docked.

Julio called to Montoya, "I see my skiff tied up here. Where is she?"

"You can't have her. I'm going to demand ransom from her rich daddy."

"I don't want her. The little bitch lies." He chuckled. "Her boyfriend killed one of my men, but I got revenge. I threw her boyfriend in the river. He probably drowned in the rapids."

Montoya stepped away from Tom. Julio turned back from tying the boat. A shocked look spread slowly over him, and he leaned over the bow rail toward Tom, ten feet in front of him on the beach. "Give him to me, Montoya. I'll kill him right now." He took his machete from his belt.

Jamie began to scream and jerk. "Don't touch him, you spineless worm. Get away from him before he kills you."

Tom's voice bellowed. It amazed her how loud he was. It must be that large muscled chest. "Come closer, Julio. I'll horsewhip you until you can't walk. How did you find out about the diamonds anyway? Tell me, because you couldn't figure it out on your own. You're not smart enough."

"You hear that, Julio?" Arturo shouted. "Nobody likes you because you're too dumb."

Jamie saw him leaning against the doorway to the wheelhouse.

"Go ashore," Arturo shouted in the loudest voice he could muster. "Get out of here so I can find my bottle. It might even be worth it to hit you over the head with it."

Montoya stood laughing at Julio and waving the stack of córdobas at him. Finally, he raised his arm to silence the shouters.

Jamie shut up. Tom and Arturo did too.

"You can have him, but if you want money for the diamonds, we have to negotiate."

Jamie thought Julio might jump over to the dock right then. He was smarter than she thought, because he studied Tom, all trussed up, and then gestured for his three men to come with him to help with the negotiations. They all had machetes in their hands. Julio stepped off the dock into the sand and walked straight up to Tom.

Jamie gasped and pulled to the end of her rope. Would he attack Tom with his machete without even a word? Julio grabbed Tom's shirt above the ropes wrapping him, and jerked him close. He laughed in Tom's face. "Now you're mine." He shook him with two hands and threw him to the sand. "Let's negotiate. I'll take care of him later."

Thank God. She stopped holding her breath.

"Good." Montoya sent his men to bring a table and two chairs. "Put the table in the shade on the east side. Bring us two Cokes so we can relax and deal." Montoya began to lead Julio and his men toward the shade.

She couldn't stand it. Tom was lying on his side, his arms pinned. He couldn't reach the gun. She pulled at the loop on her hand to run to him.

Tom wriggled. She stopped with her hand on the loop of rope restraining her. Tom rolled his body over and sat up with his back straight and his knees bent in front of him. He pulled his feet close in to his buttocks, and with an incredible feat of strength, pulled his weight up over his feet and stood. Jamie's jaw hung open. She swayed, giddy with admiration. His weight-lifting must have given him the strength. She pulled the rope loop from her hand, picked up Arturo's machete lying beside her as Tom slipped out of the coils of rope around him. She ran across the beach when all the other men had their backs to her, setting up the table in the shade of the warehouse. The evening sun made long shadows. They reminded her why she had to hurry.

Carrying his bottle, Arturo carefully climbed down to the dock and limped heavily across the sand to Tom. Tom raised a trembling hand with the pistol into the air. Looking at Jamie coming toward him, Tom shot into the sky. The explosion shattered the air, and, for a moment, the world stopped, paralyzed.

Tom dropped the pistol onto the sand, as if it burnt him, ran the few steps to Jamie, took Arturo's machete, and raced across the beach to the clanging of the large knives in the battle beginning in the shade where men shouted and roiled, moving to positions to strike each other.

Jamie put her arm under Arturo and took the weight of the wounded man on her shoulders. She started for the safety of the warehouse. Arturo dug in his feet and pointed to the gun. "Pick it up. We'll kill a couple of them."

He sagged against her and she had to let him fall when she picked up the warm weapon.

She followed Montoya's brief instructions and used two hands to shoot the pistol in the air. Again the explosion ripped her ears and almost knocked her over with the kick. "Stop!" she yelled. The battle of the eight men stopped. "Get the ropes and tie them up," she ordered, realizing her power. They were truly frightened by the gun. *I am afraid of it too.* She walked toward them, holding the gun out in front of her, her hands still shaking, ready to shoot them if they moved. "Julio, Juan, and you other two guys, drop your machetes, or I'll shoot you. Tom, get the rope and tie them up."

Out of the corner of her eye she saw Tomàs' truck pull up. The men in the shade couldn't see it. She walked closer, pointing the pistol at the stupid fighting men. *I'll stop them. I won't have to shoot anybody.* Tom ran to get the rope. She stopped in front of the men. "Don't anyone move, or I'll shoot." The pistol was heavy and her arm drooped.

Julio took his chance and jumped toward her. He slammed into her as she raised the gun, and it went off right next to her ear. Her breath filled with a sickening sulfurous smell. Her ribs hurt from the impact. He screamed something, let go of her, and backed away shuddering. She couldn't hear. She saw the hatred on his face as he fell. She dropped the gun and slid to her knees, staring at the pistol. *I didn't want to kill him. I don't think—*

Tom threw the rope to Montoya as the policeman

and Tomàs arrived. She didn't notice until Tom put his arms around her and lifted her to her feet, holding her and comforting her as silent tears rolled down her cheeks. She could hear Tom whispering in her left ear, but her right ear was completely deaf.

Arturo was talking to the policeman and pointing to Julio bleeding to death at her feet. She pulled away from Tom and knelt beside Julio. "I'm sorry." She hoped she wasn't shouting.

Tom pulled her up and whispered "hospital" in her left ear.

Tomàs, the policeman and Montoya's men carried Julio to the bed of the truck. The little boy was watching from the window of the truck. She wondered what he had learned. "It was an accident!" she shouted toward the truck. She didn't want the boy to learn that violence solved problems. She began to come out of her daze, as Montoya's men led Julio's men to the truck bed.

Tom pointed to Arturo and shook Tomàs' hand. He waved to Montoya and checked his watch. *Uncle James. Six thirty-five already.* Tom pointed down the road south and she heard him holler, "Let's go."

She ran with him, her feet clopping on the paved road. He turned into the driveway of a large one-story hotel built in dark wood. A cell tower and jungle rose behind it. They clambered up the steps and entered a lobby paneled in dark wood, with rag rugs and small wood chairs without upholstery scattered about. Tom showed his cell phone to the deskman who pointed to a small room at the side of the lobby set up for telephoning. They pushed past a Chinese man in a business suit sitting at a table with papers lying around him.

Jamie flopped into a chair, panting, and dialed, putting the phone on speaker. It took two or three minutes. Uncle James's sat phone probably had enough charge left to take the call, if he still had it on. She put the phone to her left ear, just in case her hearing wasn't good enough yet in the other.

"Hello?"

"Uncle James?" She put the phone on the table so Tom could hear.

"Why are you shouting? Is something happening that kept you from calling on time?"

"No, everything's fine now. Tom, tell him about the helicopter."

"Uncle James, we reserved the helicopter for a week. We will be in Quito at the latest six days from now, on Wednesday, the second of September. How are things at your end? "

"Not too good. The wise man, Chimbi, is very anxious for me to leave. He keeps getting threatening messages from the Sumolu. It's almost funny. The two tribes communicate by shouting across a field at each other, but it's better than the past when they just battled and the winners got the women. So I will leave early. My friends here will walk the twenty miles with me. I'll get to Machazo by Saturday if I leave the day after tomorrow."

"How many baskets of samples are you bringing? I remember the bunch you had the last time you came home. Will they fit in the helicopter?" She tried not to shout, but wasn't sure whether she was.

"I have twenty baskets, but they can be crushed anywhere. Don't worry. They'll fit. Do you hear that static? I have to hang up. The battery's about dead. Looking forward to seeing you. Bye." He ended the call as the static drowned him out.

She leaned back in her chair, utterly exhausted. "We did get here in time, didn't we?"

"Yes. It wasn't easy." He rubbed his cheek. "My mouth is really dry. I'm definitely dehydrated from the walk through the jungle. It's so hot and still under the trees. Tomàs's wife gave me some water, but I need about a gallon more and ten hours of sleep."

She laughed at Tom's appearance. "You need a shower and clean clothes."

He looked down and nodded. "And you need a rest after stealing that skiff and shooting Julio, even if it was an accident. How's your hearing?"

"Almost back. My chest hurts a bit. I think we need a room in this fancy eco-hotel—with one bed."

Tom's eyes lit up. "Absolutely." He glanced at the Chinese man still hard at work with his eyes down. Tom ran his hand through her hair and gave her a quick kiss. "We can make the call to the government in the morning, and go see Arturo in the hospital. I hope he's well enough to get us back to San Carlos. The faster we get to Managua the better." He rubbed his stubbled chin. "If we leave here tomorrow we can get paid on Friday and fly to Ecuador on Saturday. The helicopter company won't take us to the Amazon valley until Monday. Uncle James will probably be safe in Machazo until we get there."

"Probably." Jamie chewed on a piece of hair. "I bet they have a nice dining room here. We can shower and get something to eat." Her stomach rumbled at the thought. *And after that we'll share the bed...*

The Chinese man looked up. "Yes, it's very good food here." His American English surprised her. She warmed with embarrassment. He had heard every word.

Tom was rather pink too, but smiled at him. "Thanks." He took her hand and led her out of the business room.

He's probably more embarrassed than I am.

Chapter 11

At Last

Screens and air conditioning and a large bed. Expensive, but well worth it, Tom thought. *Perfect for the first night with Jamie. A beautiful room for a beautiful woman. I want it to be good for her.* He felt his body warming to what he had wanted for so many weeks, and she wanted it too. "Wait for me, darling."

He shucked his clothes on the way to the bathroom. The water was hot. For the first time since leaving Virginia, the hotel had heated water. Real luxury.

He felt a hand on his back and whirled around. Jamie stood before him naked, the tips of her beautiful breasts bright pink.

"May I come in?" she asked, one hand on the linen shower curtain and the other on his hip.

The heat of her hand spread a fire through his body. She massaged his hip. His manhood rose at the sight of her and he reached to draw her under the running water. "My darling." His arms went around her and he clung to her, body to body, with the water streaming onto their faces. At last. She streamed little kisses on his neck and shoulders and chest. An involuntary "mmm" came out of him at each kiss. "Let me look at you." He pushed her away so he could see her blue Irish eyes, shining with water on her lashes. Knowing nothing would stop this slowed him. He wanted to sear into his memory every touch of this final commitment. He tipped her head up and kissed her lips, her eyes, her ears. "I want you forever," he whispered into her soft cheek.

"This is me, Tom," she said in a serious tone. "Do you like my breasts?" Lifting them, she did a little twirl with the steamy water increasing the heat around them. The rosy peaches invited him to bend to her to cup them in his hands, to hold them, to touch the red tips. She swayed in front of him. "Tom, when you touch me, I feel so weak. You won't let me fall, will you?"

He scooped her into his arms again, one hand creeping to her breast, kneading it and the other caressing up and down her spine. She was finally letting him do what he had longed to do. He would give her everything. When he touched the nipple again, her breath hitched. He twisted slightly and her weight sank onto his arm. Her breath grew ragged.

She wants, needs me as much as I need her. He hardened even more and knew he wouldn't, couldn't, stop. He breathed in deeply and dared to slip his hands around her buttocks and into her pussy until the tips of his fingers became his entire sensual world. He lifted her and leaned her against the wall, her legs wrapped around him; he wanted to settle her on his cock. He wanted inside her, so hard and so urgent. "I can't stop, Jamie," he cried, his fingertips circling the little nub at her wet center, ready to explode.

"Don't stop, don't stop."

Her fingers dug into his back, and she moaned when he shoved into her. She tightened around him as he pumped, electricity building, finally reaching overload. He poured his semen into her, his muscles giving her all he had.

A rising moan came from her and she tightened around him.

He slowed, gripping her so she wouldn't fall, his panting bringing him back to the world, and he let her down to the shower floor. He rubbed her wet black hair and looked at her dripping face with her cheeks loose, her eyes closed.

"I love you."

She didn't answer for a moment, her hands loosening her grip on his arms. Finally she looked up and a great sob shook her and she leaned into him. "I never cried from happiness before," she mumbled into his chest.

Heat rushed through him again. *I'll never let you go. I like this part of me.*

The water cooled to lukewarm. He took the washcloth and lathered it with the scented soap and gently began to wash her body. Not bothering with the cloth, she soaped him up all over, slowing to a crawl when she came to his cock. Eventually she finished washing and rinsing him.

"I don't know whether I want to eat or to sleep or to make love again in the bed."

He pulled her close again, kissing her with a tenderness he didn't know he had in him. "Let's do it all, woman—again and again."

"Wipe that lecherous grin off your face, Mr. Conqueror. I hate to end this beautiful view of you, but we will need to cover up your magnificent appendage to eat in the dining room. Put your clothes on and let's get some of that good food."

"Okay, but you have to promise not to be embarrassed if I stare at you with my lecherous grin during dinner, señorita."

She laughed. "Likewise, I'm sure, señor."

At dinner, Tom was suddenly shy. What did she think about him? Had any of her ideas about him changed? He wasn't sure what her reaction was to succumbing to the physical temptation at last. She was so stubborn, and yet so wonderfully spirited. Her cheeks were red where his unshaven stubble had scraped her. He avoided talking about their future together.

Tom told her about the terrible heat and humidity of the jungle and she told him about how Arturo had initiated the plan for her escape. He pulled his hand away from hers every time the waiter approached. He wasn't sure how much he could show her what he was feeling. He wanted to live with this forever. They talked about going back to school, medicinal plants, mosquitoes and the Nicaraguan Miskito Indians after which they were named.

As the conversation slowed, Tom yawned. "My mother will probably tell you the tale someday about me and the mashed potatoes. I guess I was about two years old. She said I had fought her about taking a nap one afternoon. When evening came, I wasn't able to stay awake and fell asleep with my face in the mashed potatoes."

Jamie's chuckle grew into a laugh.

"It's true. I might fall asleep in the rice right now, but we have to talk about getting back to Managua."

"I know what you mean. That bed is so inviting. I guess the first thing we have to do tomorrow morning is to get the papers signed by Montoya. I hope he doesn't give us any trouble."

"Don't worry. I have that taken care of. I have the threat of taking his smuggling operations to the police, and he has the threat of telling the police that I knew about the guns and sent them off anyway. Actually, the first thing I'll do is call the New York coast guard. I think they are the ones that handle smuggling. If by chance, we have a problem getting to the right organization, I'll call the Department of Homeland Security. They will know who to contact. I will tell them Roberto Estrella is responsible."

She frowned. "We do have to go to the hospital to see if Arturo can take us back. I'd like to check on Julio too. I hope I didn't kill him."

He squeezed her hand. *She really is worried about it. Just like me. All this violence...* "We didn't know we were going to fight for our own lives, Jamie. It's worth it for Uncle James, isn't it?"

She looked confused for a moment. "Yes, but I'm tired of being scared, and fighting. I guess I'm just tired, too." She smiled up at him. "At least I have you."

He melted inside. "Forever." He pulled himself back on track. "We have to get to Managua as fast as we can to get paid before the smugglers arrive in New York. If Arturo can't take us back, maybe the passenger boat can. I don't think it is fast enough, though. It probably takes longer to go up river than down. We'll find out tomorrow."

As Tom started to rise from the table, he turned and almost bumped into the Chinese man.

"Excuse me for interrupting. Perhaps I can help."

Tom frowned. "Oh?"

He gave a slight bow to Jamie and sat down close to Tom. "I understand that you are going to report Montoya's smuggling."

Tom's throat contracted. He felt strangled. *How does he know? Is he listening to everything we say?* "Uhh, yes."

"It is better you report it to your government than I report it to the Nicaraguan government. I am Wu Cheng, the representative of the Chinese government in this town. My job is to supervise the beginning of the canal we are building from here to the Pacific coast. If I report the smuggling, the Nicaraguan Government might take weeks to argue about whether they can get bribe money out of me or Montoya before they decide that the new canal is more important. I understand that you are in a hurry to get to Quito, Ecuador, to rescue an uncle? That is where I can help."

Tom's spirit rose. "How can you help?"

"It is tedious and slow to have to take boats to Managua from here. I have a small plane that I use to fly directly to Managua when I have business in the city. If you pay me for the gas, I will let you rent my plane and my pilot to fly to Managua. It would save you several days."

Jamie hung on Tom's arm now. "Why would you do that for us? Why do you want to get rid of the smugglers?"

"This is a small town. It will expand soon. New businesses will develop. We will be building a larger airport. Thousands of laborers will come to work for the engineers already here. We will build roads to bring in materials. We will build factories and houses for the people we hire to help us build. People who own land or businesses along the canal will get rich."

Tom looked at Jamie. "Mamacita. Arturo. Captain Ricardo."

"Did you know that the Nicaraguan Government has changed the official name of this town from San Juan del Norte to San Juan de Nicaragua?" the man continued. "All because of the canal we are building. We do not need smugglers in this port. They will be caught and the government will slow economic development with its irregular and slow court system. Believe me, I don't want a crime-ridden town here. We will have five policemen by next year, and more after that. If I help you, you will be helping me." He stopped talking and scrutinized them. "Tell me about yourselves, and why you are involved with the smugglers."

Tom's mind raced, adrenaline waking him up one more time today. The man certainly had a long-term view. Even if the canal never went through, Tom admired his intelligence and impressive plan. Very Chinese, he thought. "I'm Tom Kirk and this is Jamie Patrick. We're from Virginia in the USA." He gave Wu an abbreviated version of their adventures. He was too tired to give details. They set two o'clock tomorrow afternoon as the time to meet the pilot at the hotel. It would cost them only three thousand córdobas, about a hundred and eight dollars, straight out of the money Estrella had given them for expenses.

Tom and Jamie talked about this incredible luck, as they changed into night clothes out of habit from living in hostel dormitories all summer. They turned out the lights, adjusted the air conditioning that they weren't used to, and climbed into bed.

Tom reached for Jamie and discovered her clothes. She giggled and shed her gown quickly. Tom stepped out of bed to remove his shorts. He climbed back in and cuddled up to her. She didn't move. On his elbow, he examined her in the dim light of the moon through the window. She was sound asleep, his beautiful woman. He cuddled around her again, sighed with deep satisfaction, and closed his eyes.

ೞೞ

Jamie sat silently in Montoya's office the next day. Tom chatted away as if Guillermo Montoya were a friend. She was too absorbed remembering the joy this morning, waking up with Tom. She had held back her desires so long this summer. Thank god, that time was over.

She had now let herself give and receive freely. She couldn't think of anything other than Tom's hands, his sucking on her breast and the impossible sense of completion when he came inside of her. She sat up straight, worried Montoya would notice her distraction.

Sitting up made her notice her sore well-used bottom and her mind was off again, feeling him pounding her. She wondered that it had been so easy to submit. She had her own ideas about pleasure for both of them, but somehow it was Tom who led the way in bed.

Warmth filled her with tenderness for this man in the chair beside her. *He's so good. I'll love him forever. He'll take care of me and I'll take care of him.*

She was distracted from her distraction when she heard Montoya say, "Give me the contract so I can sign it. You've certainly earned your pay. Thank you for saving the crates from those thieves."

He was a dangerous man, a smuggler. Why should he thank them? She dug into her backpack to bring out her contract and set it on the desk beside Tom's.

They had discussed the canal and how it would affect Montoya's "business," if it actually went through. Tom advised him to switch to something legal.

"I might, after this job is over. Don't forget to tell

Estrella that I'm through with him, but wait until you have your pay. You deserve it."

Jamie wondered how Tom could lie so well to Montoya's face, when he didn't know how to lie a few days ago. Didn't he feel guilty? It was one thing to lie about her being pregnant as he had on the lake ferry. *Oooh. Pregnant.* She thought about the possibility. Well, if she were, it would make her happy. They would get married when they got home. Anyway, it was quite another thing to let Montoya think he was safe, and would soon be in possession of a million dollars. That was ridiculous when she thought about it. She couldn't imagine that the guns were worth more than five hundred thousand. Montoya would never get any money. The coast guard would pick up the submarine before it even approached New York. They had assured Tom when he called. How soon would Montoya or Estrella get the news? Her chest tightened. *We have to get out of Nicaragua as fast as we can. Either one of them might kill us if they find out before we leave.*

Tom stood and shook Montoya's hand.

She picked up her contract and stood too, anxious to go. She opened her pack to put the contract in. As she folded it she saw that Montoya had not signed hers. She interrupted their goodbyes. "Sign my contract, Señor Montoya."

He apologized at once and signed it. *Too smooth for my taste. He probably ignored me deliberately because I'm a woman. How can Tom treat him like a friend?* They walked back to the hotel and asked the man at the counter to call a taxi for them. The hospital was on the other side of town, almost out in the countryside. She wanted to ask Tom about how he decided who to trust. Did he listen to his gut like she listened to hers? At least neither of them had trusted Julio.

When Tom asked her why she was so quiet, she put him off. She would talk to him later, after they saw Arturo.

At the hospital, Arturo delighted her by standing when they walked in. "I'm getting my strength back," he crowed. "This is my second and last pint—of blood, not whiskey. They took my bottle away," he grumbled, hanging onto the stand that held the bag of blood. "No shakes for me if I take my medicine. I'm doing okay. They even said my leg looked good. When are we leaving?"

"Sorry, old man," Tom said. "Nothing I'd like better than taking a leisurely trip back up the river with you. You know we're in a hurry though, and the Chinese man who's in charge of getting the canal work going in this town offered us a plane ride to Managua. We fly in two hours."

Arturo's face fell. Jamie reached for him and gave him a hug. "I promise we'll come back to visit you and Mamacita, maybe on our honeymoon."

"I knew it. Your faces look different, more relaxed. Tom, you're a lucky man to catch this woman. Don't lose her in the Amazon."

Tom grinned. "She's the best."

"Tom, will you give me a few minutes alone with Arturo? I want to ask him something."

He raised his eyebrows. "Sure. I'll wait in the hall-way."

After she closed the door behind him, Arturo wagged his finger at her. "You better treat him well, girl. You aren't lying to him, are you?"

"Oh, no. I just need your advice." She wriggled where she sat on the bed, not sure how to say it.

"Ask away, you pretty thing, though I'm not exactly a fount of wisdom."

"Well, you've always been respectful to me, and we can talk about anything, and you're a man. Maybe you can help me."

He nodded.

She took a deep breath. "Thank you, Arturo. Every other man I've met in Nicaragua is surprised that I have anything to say. They all seem to take it for granted that Tom is the one to talk to, to make arrangements with, to decide things. They never even look at me unless I inter-rupt. They treat me as if I'm worthless."

"Lots of men are like that in Nicaragua. The man is in charge and controls his woman. What do you want to know?"

She was beginning to think she sounded silly, but she spilled it out anyway. "I think that Tom doesn't care that other men expect me to be a mouse. He didn't even no-tice that Montoya didn't bother to sign my contract until I pointed it out. Sometimes Tom tells me what to do. I don't like it." Her face flamed suddenly as she remem-bered loving how he had controlled her last night and this morning.

Arturo guessed what she was thinking, because he winked at her. "But not always, eh? Part of you likes it when he tells you what to do, I bet. Well, just wait a few years, little lady. You'll find that you have to give a little, and he has to give a little."

"A few years?"

"Yes, it takes that long. Now, you go to Tom. I'll see you again sometime. You made me think about visiting Mamacita." He hugged her and shoved her toward the door.

How could she have come to love him in three days? She opened the door with a lump in her throat. "No more bottles of whiskey, old man. I want you to be in good shape when I come back. Bye."

She grabbed Tom's hand and headed toward the stairs down to the first floor, her throat full of unsaid things.

"I thought you wanted to check on Julio. I asked at the nurses' station. He'll survive. Your bullet didn't break any bones."

She stopped. "Good. He'll have a day in court. I'm so ashamed that I almost killed him. I'm not entirely sure that I didn't want to. It scares me, what I did. I keep seeing that look of hate he gave me after I did it." She hesitated, and then admitted, "Maybe I deserved it." She hurried out the front door, looking for the taxi.

Chapter 12

But She Leaves

Wu introduced them to the pilot and sent them off after he counted their money.

The airfield was just that, a pasture surrounded by tilled land. The single engine plane was in the air within five minutes. Jamie tried to put everything out of her mind, but she kept rocketing between the joy of surrendering last night and the resentment of men controlling her. She did enjoy the view of the jungle and the rolling grasslands that trees had covered before the revolution.

The pilot pointed out a volcano with smoke rising from it as they passed Granada, and a gorgeous blue lake nestled in an old volcanic cauldron. They flew over Managua and landed on the far side of the airport. It was six o'clock and the sun was setting.

Their taxi hurried through the darkening streets to

Estrella's office and pulled up in front of the two guards at the iron-barred gate.

She paid the taxi fare, knowing it was too much, and asked him to wait, hoping the business wouldn't take too long. She wanted to get this over with. When she turned from the taxi, Tom steered her toward one of the guards. After Tom reminded him that they had left with a load of crates just four days ago, the guard ran up the stairs. While they waited, she said good evening to the other guard, but Tom jerked her around.

She was not in the mood for Tom to tell her that she shouldn't talk to the other guard. Before she objected, he pulled her across the courtyard to meet the guard coming down the stairs with a flashlight for them.

"Tom," she said, in a lilting tone that wouldn't let him know that she was angry, "why didn't you want me to talk to the guard?"

He stopped on the narrow and dark metal stairs, the flashlight lighting the ceiling above them. "I think I recognize that guard, the one with the cleft chin. He looks like the twin of one of Montoya's men."

She opened her mouth to say it didn't matter. Then the implications began to choke her. "Oh my god, I wonder if Estrella knows."

"Let's not say anything about him at first. Let's just tell Estrella all that happened on the trip, and get our money. Then we can wonder how Julio found out about the diamonds. We'll wait to see his reaction. If Estrella doesn't figure it out we'll mention that his guard must be the twin brother of one of Montoya's men. Then we'll get out as fast as we can."

"Sounds scary, but we need the cash." Her stomach tightened. *We'll get to the jungle in time.* She remembered her uncle comforting her when she had a cut knee. *Now he needs me.*

Jamie followed Tom up the stairs, glancing over the balcony railing at the crates below. She shuddered at the thought of what might be in them. What would a cell in New York City do with more rocket launchers? *I pray the FBI can stop them.* Her shallow breathing deepened as she marched into the light of Estrella's office. Who was he to decide that it was okay to blow up innocent people with deadly weapons?

She thought then that Estrella might have a boss. Who had given him the guns to transport to New York? It was too much. Let the coast guard or Homeland Security figure it out.

She followed Tom into the office, aware that she might be involved in an international problem. She wanted her money and she wanted out.

The fat sleazy man was still wearing the too short tie. He shook their hands before they sat. Tom threw the van keys on the desk and explained where the van was.

Jamie took the signed contract and slammed it on the desk. "Give us our pay. Please. We earned it. Show him your contract, Tom."

Estrella took his eyes from Tom and looked at her. "Let's talk about it first, little lady."

Tom laid his hand on her arm, but she burst out,

"No! Give us our cash first. Be honest and keep our agreement."

Tom's grip on her arm tightened.

Estrella frowned, took out a crumpled tissue and blew his nose, probably to delay answering.

She waited.

He shook his head. "Tell me what happened."

She was shaking inside. "No. Give us our money, or we'll take these contracts to the police." She reached over and picked up the two papers, folded them carefully, and stuffed them in her pack.

Estrella slammed his hand on the desk. "*Puta*! Tell me what happened!"

Tom jumped to his feet at the insult to Jamie. His hand on her shoulder kept her sitting. "She's right, Estrella," he said calmly. "Give us the cash. Otherwise we'll go to the government. You can't bribe officials about this because they have to bow to the wishes of the Chinese government if they want the canal. They won't allow smuggling."

The fat man leaned back, pretending to be surprised. "Smuggling? What smuggling? We sent diamond cores and you know it."

Disgusting. "Don't be obtuse, Estrella," she growled. Tom's hand kept her sitting.

"Obtuse? What is this word?"

Tom leaned over the desk and grabbed the short tie. "Don't lie to us, you bastard. We won't tell you what we know until you give us the cash."

Estrella pulled his tie out of Tom's hand. Pretending

to be insulted, he huffed. "If you insist on being so impolite and crude just because I asked what happened, I'll give you the cash." He stood, and studied each of them with a frown. "And then you will tell me everything that you know."

Behind him was a two meter tall safe with the heavy door hanging open. He swung the door wider and took out two bundles of cash. "Each of these is a thousand dollars, just what we agreed." He handed them to Tom.

Tom handed them to Jamie. "That's for Jamie and all that she went through for you, including your insults. She earned it. Now give me the same. This was not the ordinary delivery and you know it."

Estrella's eyes bulged. He opened his mouth and closed it. He reached into the safe again and threw another two bundles onto the desk.

Tom calmly put them in his pack and sat down. "Tell him what happened, Jamie. Every detail. Then we'll leave him to figure out his own problems."

Intensely relieved, Jamie flashed Tom a big smile. She would love him forever. He certainly could handle these Nicaraguan men. She sat back and told their story, beginning with Captain Ricardo and the fight with Julio.

"Who is Julio?"

"A guy who found out about the diamond cores."

Jamie continued with the discovery of the military hardware.

Estrella tapped the desk. "So you found the guns."

"Yes, and we avoided the coastal guards so that we didn't have to tell them, because we need the cash you paid us to rescue my uncle." She yearned to tell him what she thought of sending rocket launchers to New York City, where terrorists would no doubt use them on innocent people. She continued, telling Estrella about the piracy and Tom's trip through the jungle, and the shooting of Julio.

Tom told Estrella how she had escaped from the barge, and that she was the one who had shot Julio.

"Congratulations, little lady. Jamie, isn't it? Apparently there's more to you than I thought."

Jamie bridled at this further insult. She opened her mouth, but snapped it shut. She wanted to leave.

To her surprise Estrella addressed her. "I have a couple of questions, Jamie. Did Julio know about the guns?"

"No. He thought he was going to get rich with the diamonds. He didn't know what to do with the raw diamonds in the brief time he had them."

He leaned toward her, squinting. "How did he find out about my diamonds? Did you tell him?"

It was the final straw. She threw herself at the desk and leaned over it. Estrella drew back.

"I'm not stupid enough to do that," she screeched into his face. "Apparently, you are. You don't even know that one of the men at your gate with the machine guns is the twin brother of one of Montoya's men. Now who do you suppose hired that maniac Julio? You figure it out. We're leaving." She turned to the doorway, taking her pack on the way.

Tom was smiling at her. "By the way, Montoya said to tell you he's through with you too." He grabbed his pack with one hand, waved goodbye to Estrella, and gave him the finger.

She heard the fat man roar as they ran across the balcony and clattered down the stairs with Estrella following them.

They burst out of the door with Estrella lumbering just behind them, and Tom ran toward the guard who was the twin, hollering to him, "Estrella's after you. Run!"

Jamie headed for the waiting taxi.

A machine gun let out a burst of bullets. She froze in her tracks. For a moment, she didn't turn, afraid the guard had shot Tom.

Oh my god, he is on the ground.

Two bodies lay in the courtyard. The skinny one was Tom. Her hand flew to her mouth, and then she moved. She bent over him searching for the wound. His left arm looked shredded, red and oozing in the courtyard lights. "Help me," she cried to the guard standing over her. They carried Tom to the taxi. "Quick, the nearest hospital." She crawled in beside him. Tom was still. Then he groaned.

❧❧❧

Tom woke to a dim room. *Hospital. My arm hurts.* White everywhere, until he saw Jamie asleep on a chair leaning on a wide windowsill. She had a pillow under her arm to soften the edge of the windowsill. He wanted to reach out to her, but he was too groggy to move. He let himself fall back to sleep. He woke again, and Jamie was still in the same position.

"Jamie," he croaked out, wanting her to wake up. She didn't move. Maybe she was only a dream. He had dreamed of her so long—all summer. Their blissful night in bed hadn't been a dream. "Jamie," he called again, wanting her to wake up, needing her. She did stir this time. "Jamie, wake up. What happened?"

She stretched, groaning, and looked at her watch. "Four o'clock in the morning. How are you feeling? The doctor only gave you a light anesthetic while he cleaned your wound. If it's hurting, they'll give you some pain-killers." She stood and sat on the edge of the bed smiling, her hair a little frowzy.

"It must not be too bad or you wouldn't be smiling. Tell me what happened."

"I don't want to think about it."

"Please tell me. I seem to be a bit foggy."

"Do you remember the conversation in Estrella's office?"

"Yes, I remember you gave him what for and then stormed out. You were great."

"When we came out in the courtyard you ran to the guard to warn him that Estrella was coming after him. You tried to stop him when he raised the machine gun to shoot around you and kill Estrella. He got the man, but grazed you in the arm with two of the bullets. You dropped like a stone, but you're really not that badly hurt. The bullets didn't even stay in your arm. You have a lovely bandage," she teased.

He looked at his left arm, the one that was hurting him. A giant white bandage covered his arm from the armpit to the elbow. He moaned. "Would you ask the nurse for some painkiller? I think I need it. Oh wait, I have to get out of here. We've got to fly to Ecuador in the morning."

"Don't worry about that. You'll be out in a couple of days if you have no fever, and we have extra time because we had that plane ride. I'll get you some painkillers right now." She kissed him lightly and left the room.

When she came back he leaned on his right elbow and took the pills "Jamie, did you get any dinner last night?"

"No. I've been here since we arrived in the taxi."

"Well, you might not like me to tell you what to do, but I'm going to tell you. Go get a taxi to that small bed and breakfast we stayed at before we went to Granada. They have a good breakfast. We have plenty of money now. You sleep for seven or eight hours and have all the breakfast you can eat before you come back here. Make sure that somebody at the desk here tells you what taxi to call so you'll be safe going to the motel at this time of night. Okay?"

She smiled. "Why don't you let me take care of you for a change? I can take care of myself."

"Do that, darling. I'll see you tomorrow."

Jamie woke him the next day with hugs and kisses.

It was almost one o'clock. That rather shocked him. "I haven't had anything to eat except pain pills since yesterday morning. I remember waking this morning sometime and asking for another one. They must be really strong."

"They are. Morphine."

"Morphine! I could get addicted. Tell them I don't want any more."

"I already did. They'll give you some Oxycodone from now on, and then only four a day. They'll give you a prescription when you leave the hospital."

"I can't get on the plane if I'm too drugged to walk." He got out of bed and walked over to the only chair in the room and sat. "I'm a little wobbly." He laughed at his weakness. "Don't worry, Jamie. I'll be all right by tomorrow. What time does the plane leave? I think it's once a day about this time."

"Right. The plane leaves at one-twenty." She looked sideways at him. "However, you won't be on it."

Tom frowned. She wouldn't do that to him, leave for Ecuador without him. "Why not?"

"Because the nurse told me this morning that even if the doctor says it's all right, you'll have to stay another day in the hospital. A policeman has to come and interview anybody who has a gunshot wound. He'll come tomorrow in the afternoon."

"Oh no. We can take the plane on Thursday. That way we'll get the helicopter and reach Machazo before Uncle James arrives on Saturday."

She chuckled. "That's a good plan, but today is Wednesday. Tomorrow is Thursday and I have to leave, but you can't leave until Friday. Don't worry about it, Tom. You can get the helicopter to take you on Saturday. I already called the helicopter company to tell them we— I—will need them on Friday instead of Monday, and then they will take you on Saturday. Everything will work out fine, since we have the 'copter for a week. The reservation is all set for a week, remember?"

Tom shook inside. How could Jamie go without him? They'd been together all summer, only apart for one afternoon the day before yesterday. Not only that, they were really committed now. "How can I protect you, if you're in a little jungle village in Ecuador without me?"

"It's not so little, Tom. It has a helicopter pad, remember? And electricity, because my uncle can charge his phone there. I know there's a store there. I'm sure someone will let me stay the night. When you come the next day in the helicopter we'll just load up Uncle James and his stuff and leave."

"What if he's not there? What if a snake bites you? What's the matter with you? You can't be a woman alone in the jungle. What kinds of men run the village? You can't go, Jamie. It's too dangerous." He could manage without her, but she couldn't manage without him.

He saw her stiffen.

"Don't tell me what I can and can't do, Tom. I'm an adult and even if I marry you, I'll always do what I want." Her voice trembled.

"I'm sure you will. I hope you'll be more sensible about what you want. You can't go larking about taking risks whenever you feel like it without thinking about what would happen to the people you love if you get hurt or die."

She sat stubbornly silent on the bed.

"Come walk with me up and down the corridors so I

can get the morphine out of my system. I need to think more clearly. Right now, I can't think about anything except what could happen to you alone in the jungle. What if you went for a walk and got bit by a poison frog?"

"Oh, Tom. Nothing like that will happen to me. Besides, frogs don't bite. Like I said, 'I'm an adult.' I can be sensible. How can you love me like you do if you think that I can't ever be alone, that I don't have brains enough to be careful when it's necessary?"

"Let's walk." Damn. He'd have to get another machete. He raised his bandaged arm toward his brow to test it and groaned. Jamie's grip on his other arm tightened. "I can use a machete with my right hand."

She fingered the bandage. "Another scar for you from a gun."

"Jamie, just because I want to protect you, it doesn't mean I'm trying to control you." It didn't work.

"You're just like my father. There's not much difference between protecting and controlling."

"I'm not your father."

"Yes, you are, if you don't trust me and my judgment. He tries to protect me to the point of suffocation. After my mom died, he started dating Marie. He wouldn't even introduce her to me for years. He thought he was 'protecting' me. He was convinced I wouldn't like her and he would have to choose between us. She's a perfectly nice woman, and I'm glad he finally married her. This trip to Europe is their honeymoon. Are you afraid to lose me if you're not with me?"

"I have to think about that one." He walked to wear

the morphine off and get back to normal. "I'm going to be miserable for weeks. I hate guns. I'd rather die than shoot one again." The thought that she would leave punched him in his midsection. "Jamie, I need to tell you. You're right about one thing. I try to control you because I'm afraid to lose you. It never works." He caught his breath. "I can't convince you not to take this risk." He cut off the rise in his voice and made one last try. "Remember when I thought the delivery job was risky because of the possibility of smuggling? You have to admit I was right about that."

She wrapped her herself around his good arm. "That doesn't mean you get to make all decisions." She pulled away and looked up at him. "It's a matter of respect. I'll only be gone one day. I love you, whether we're together or apart. Goodnight now. See you on Saturday." She leaned up and kissed him on his lips.

Holding her back wouldn't work. He forced his twitching fingers to his side. He had to respect her decision. He churned inside. She waved goodbye. A slow burn filled his stomach and his head. He pounded the mattress and leaped up. *How can she do this to me?*

What would he find when he got to Ecuador? *I might never see her again. Am I losing her?* He fell back on the bed as she walked out.

Chapter 13

Captured

The village filled a cleared space beside the Tinoca branch of the Amazon, where it flowed down the eastern slopes of the Andes. Jamie jumped down from the helicopter, out from under the blades, and stopped to catch her breath. Her feet sank into the damp earth, and she breathed in misty air. Two men approached, one in a pair of red shorts, and the other in pink lace women's panties.

She held back her chuckle. Surely someone would explain. Their smooth brown bodies had a yellowish cast and the colors all seemed too bright. A generator chugged in the background.

As soon as the rotors stopped she felt the heat sit on her like a weight.

She stepped forward to greet them, hoping her Spanish would suffice. Red shorts waved to the helicopter pilot and shouted in Spanish to come back in four days. He came uncomfortably close to her.

"Buenos dias, señorita. You are Jamie, the doctor's niece? I am Samal, the storekeeper." He gestured toward the one large building of uncut logs with a tin roof. The store, several smaller huts, and a wharf with a rusty motorboat tied to it, comprised the "town." The green bushes and trees of jungle surrounded it a hundred feet away.

She nodded.

Whew! A lot smaller than she anticipated. Jarred at the unexpected rawness, she glanced around for people with more clothes on. "Where is my Uncle James? Not here yet?"

Pink panties said something in another language to her while leaning on his spear. He had six-inch pieces of bone piercing his ears, and white spots painted on his cheeks. He stared openly at her and reached out to touch her arm with a finger.

Although startled at the intimacy, she didn't jerk back. Who knew what behavior to expect here?

"This is Koti of the Walaka Indians," Samal said. "He will explain to you about Uncle James."

She caught her breath and squinted at Samal. "Explain? What's wrong?"

"Come. We will wait in the shade. Take the chair for you by the tree." He pointed to a plastic green yard chair of the kind ubiquitous world-wide.

Too enervated to be comfortable, she sat anyway, and Samal disappeared into the store to bring her something to drink.

Koti squatted in front of her, one hand on his ten foot spear, which had no point at the end. It was a blowgun. Seeing too much through the panties she pulled her shirt down to make sure she was covered.

Koti surprised her again when he spoke in Spanish looking up at her. "Do not worry. Your uncle is on his way to this town. He is not here yet because he walked on the wrong path. He is here in our lands for many years, but still he makes mistakes." His brown eyes crinkled above the spots.

"I *am* worried. What is the problem?" She didn't like being above him in the chair, so she slid off onto her knees on the ground in front of him.

He smiled and the spots on his cheeks moved. He used the bottom end of his blowgun to draw a line in the red dirt. "This is the path, and this is a tree beside the path. A large root from the tree crosses the path. The doctor steps over the root instead of onto the root. He does not see the hole on the other side. He turns back to speak to me and he loses balance." Koti's arms swung wide, blowgun waving above his head. "He bangs head onto tree and breaks ankle. Now he does not walk."

"Oh no…" She rocked back on her heels, her head stuffed with sand, her thinking muffled. "What can I do? He must be in terrible pain." She leaned forward and wrapped her fingers on his warm arm. "I must help him."

"Yes, we help him now. We tie two bamboo poles together at one end and put net of vines across other end. We put doctor on net and pull. We carry over roots and around trees, but very slow. We happy we have machetes from Samal and government. Doctor arrives here tomorrow. I come in front. Wait here for you."

"I am very happy you are helping him." She leaned closer yet and looked into his brown eyes, both hands on his arms now. His face was so open. She wanted to trust him. "You are a good man. Walaka Indians are good people to my uncle."

Koti smiled and his left arm rose to hers.

They were kneeling with their arms clinging when Samal came out with canned soda and bottled water for them.

What do I do now? If Tom were here, he would tell me what to do. She drank the water down swiftly, surprised at how thirsty she was in this wet climate. *I need to make my own decisions. I need to take care of Uncle James, like he took care of me.*

"Samal, can I go out to meet my uncle? I could walk beside him and try to help him feel better and forget the pain until we get some painkiller medicine for him, until we can get his ankle set. I am not afraid," she added, watching Koti for his reaction.

Koti looked up at the sun. Jamie glanced at her watch. Three in the afternoon.

Samal pointed at her watch. "Yes, it is too late to leave today. Perhaps you should wait for him here."

Koti took a feathered dart from the pack at his waist and inserted it in the blowgun. He aimed the ten foot long pole at some invisible creature in a nearby treetop and blew. "The warriors from the Sumolu tribe can be near in the jungle now," he explained. "They do not want to wait.

This is good hunting season. More dry. Also camu camu harvest already begins. They are afraid of the doctor shaman."

He was very clear. She took her kerchief from her pocket and wiped the sweat from her warm face. "Samal, do you have a machete that you can sell me? I will want to protect myself when I go."

Samal shook his head. "I do not like this. You cannot protect against a blowgun, or even a bow and arrow, with a machete. The dart from a blowgun will not kill you, but it will make you sick for a long time."

It might be foolhardy, but I need to get to Uncle James.

She heard a thump. Under the tree where he had blown the dart, Koti was picking up a limp spider monkey. "This is my food." He walked to the nearest hut.

Jamie crossed the raised wood threshold into the crowded store and bought a machete, some canned sardines, and some soggy crackers. Samal told her she could not go into the jungle alone, so she considered it. Munching on her dinner she stood staring at the small trail leading west that Samal had indicated led to her uncle.

I'm not stupid enough to go into the jungle alone.

She wandered around the village. The decrepit looking motorboat had *The Saviour* painted by hand on the side. Probably Samal used it to bring trade goods to the store.

A naked man with a net climbed from one of the canoes at the edge of the river. He stared and waved two fish and a turtle at her. *I guess he's not afraid of pira-*

nhas. A monkey in the tree overhead startled her with its howl and the fisherman laughed at her.

She watched two women shaping clay masks to put in the fire pit in front of them. When she picked one up and held it to her face they shook their heads no. It was too large for her. She laughed too when they gestured that the masks were for a man, and not for a woman. A finished mask had eyebrows made of feathers, white spots and red lips. Not exactly beautiful. She supposed they meant to scare people with jagged purple streaks and the pointy teeth painted in yellow.

Two three-year-old boys, tied by their ankles to a nearby tree, played with a monkey she assumed was a pet. It was nearly dark when she waved goodbye to the women and headed to the store to ask Samal for a place to sleep for the night.

Koti appeared beside her and gave her a jolt. No longer the friendly brown man in pink panties, he wore a woven grass cone over his penis tied to a thong around his hips. The wide jaguar pelt with its beautiful black rosettes on orange wove around his waist. It held an axe as well as his pouch of darts and a quiver of arrows. A bow swung over his shoulders. The white of the bones in his ear lobes glinted. The naked warrior stomped his blowgun in the ground. "We go now."

"But it's dark," came out of her mouth in a squeal.

"This is good time. Sumolu warriors not come at night. They are afraid. I am not afraid. Pick up your pack."

She swallowed and decided. She wasn't afraid either,

if he wasn't. Just nervous. "One moment."

Samal sold her a leather belt to hold her machete. He explained Koti had worn the pink panties because he wanted her to be happy, not frightened. "He is a kind man, but sometimes he is too brave. Señorita, do not go into the trees tonight."

"I am going." She wanted to tell him what she had been through in Nicaragua for Uncle James, but she didn't have time.

"You are too brave also."

She hoisted her pack to her shoulder and followed Koti to the dark shadows beneath the trees and bushes. It was black. Very black. She put one hand on his warm shoulder and walked forward onto the trail padded with rotten leaves.

Jamie concentrated on not losing her balance as she worked her way over the uneven levels of the path in the dark. After an hour of constant stumbling she figured out how to slide her feet over the ground's changing leaf thickness.

Koti whispered warnings about surface roots under-foot. After her eyes adjusted to the pitch black she dropped her hand and followed the warmth of his back as they wound down the narrow trail.

Guttural humphs, croaks and high-pitched squeaks floated in the heavy air around them. Frog and insect voices, no doubt. She heard a snarl next to her hand and jerked back instinctively from the branch. Koti reached to take her arm and they continued.

When they crossed the river as it bent to the south,

Koti led the way wading between stones. She clung to his shoulder as the water rose to her waist, but he continued steadily. *He must not be worried about piranhas.*

Back on the path, hours passed and Jamie's muscles tired from the balancing footwork.

Koti stopped, arms outstretched. "We will go around," he whispered. "A net lies in the path." He silently pushed the stalk of a large-leafed plant behind him and his heat disappeared.

Stay calm. She followed and staggered, cracking a branch beneath her. Koti stood solid in front of her. They listened. Nothing. Two more quiet steps and they listened again. A few more steps and Koti stepped back onto the trail.

She heard an "unnh." He grabbed his left arm.

She reached for him and stumbled to the uneven ground feeling the cross-hatch of a net beneath her. She screamed as it closed over her, and then she was dragged face down, scraping the ground for a few feet, and dropped.

She struggled to reach her machete but it was too tangled.

Koti shouted, "*Hui!*" Run.

It was too late. With a desperate screech she tried to tear apart the net. The knots would not move. She heard a gurgling scream from either Koti or the attacker. She fought some more for her machete, but the attacker swooped up the net and she was dangling from his shoulder upside down.

Her head kept bumping into something. The warmth

of Koti's bare leg hung beside her, slippery with blood. "Oh, god…" she wailed.

The attacker was carrying them both away from the path into the deep untracked jungle.

ↄ∽ↄ

Tom ran out from under the vanes of the helicopter despite the throbbing underneath the bandage on his arm. A man in red shorts ran over and introduced himself as Samal. Tom's eyes wandered over the small enclave of huts. He shook his head at the false picture Jamie had painted of it. Where was she?

Samal waved the helicopter away and shouted over the noise, "Come with me."

Tom hurried after him into the store. *No Jamie. What is going on?* "Where is Jamie Patrick? The helicopter pilot brought her here yesterday."

Samal waved his arms. "I don't know. I advised her not to leave. She didn't listen. She left last night."

She left? He didn't hear anymore as it tore through him. He stumbled against a table, catching himself with his left hand. "Shit!" He grabbed his forearm and held it close against his body while the pain tore through. "What happened?" he ground out between clenched teeth.

"Sit down. Her uncle, the doctor who was coming here from the Walaka tribe, fell and broke his ankle on the way here. The Indians sent one of the wise man's sons on ahead of the group to let Jamie Patrick know that they would get him here by tomorrow." Samal walked

back and forth between the loaded tables. He looked upset and was talking loud.

Tom grabbed him. "Where is she?"

Samal slumped. "I didn't think she would leave. I'm
sorry I didn't tell her why it was so dangerous," he explained in a low voice, staring at the floor. "Yesterday
afternoon she wanted to go meet her uncle in the jungle
on the trail so she could comfort him, make him feel better, because he must be in pain. I told her it was too late
in the day and she should wait here for her uncle. She
seemed to relax all afternoon, but when it got dark, Koti,
the wise man's son, convinced her to leave with him. He
must have thought it was safer than in the daytime. They
left last night about six o'clock when it was dark." He
looked up from his bent head. "Maybe she found her uncle by—"

Tom cut him off. "You let her go into the jungle in
the middle of the night? A girl from a big city?" He
pounded his fist into his thigh, the burn pushing him to
act. The words spilled out quickly. "We have to go out to
find them. I can't wait here. I need to be certain she's
safe." The anger burst out. "How could she be so stupid?
I'll have to marry her to keep her safe." He knew that was
the wrong thing to say, but the instinct inside him was
turning in his brain. He grabbed a machete from the shelf
and dragged Samal after him. "C'mon."

⁏⁊⁊⁊

She woke on damp ground with tears running down

her cheeks. Her eyes opened and followed a rope from her ankle to a narrow tree trunk three feet away.

I'm alive. He didn't kill me. Yet.

Koti lay beside her, maybe dead, with his legs stretched out and covered with blood. Jamie bawled aloud, but choked it back when a man turned at the sound. He crouched beside a pile of bamboo poles. She trembled when he left off shaping the ends of the poles and walked to her carrying a small axe.

She wiped her cheeks. The shaking inside got worse as she stood to face her captor. Tall and thin, with the same yellowish coffee skin of Koti, he was dressed, or undressed, differently than the Walaka Indian. His hair had blue feathers in a band around his head above the ears. The macaw feathers hung from his ears also, and from his penis cone. His nose had a small bone, almost like a white mustache, angled down on each side. Somehow the white spots painted on his cheeks were not so friendly.

Like Koti and Samal, he came uncomfortably close, staring at her skin. When he reached out to touch it, she understood in the moment that he had never seen someone with Caucasian skin, tanned though it was from the tropical sun. "Sumolu?" she asked, and he jumped back two feet, apparently surprised she spoke.

He nodded and studied her face. She pointed to Koti on the ground. "Walaka." The man frowned, and shook his axe at the still body. *Oh god, I hope he isn't dead.* She pointed to herself. "American."

He questioned with his eyes. "American," she repeated.

"Amelicanu?"

She nodded. So far so good. She pointed again. "Walaka, Koti. American, Jamie. Sumolu?"

After a short hesitation, he drew straight. "Sumolu. Anakoli." He broke into a speech waving his arms, pounding his chest. "Shaman," he shouted.

"Shaman?"

When she stepped back, he took a large pouch from his waist band of brown skin, took a small sack from it and waved it at her. Did he mean shaman, as in medicine man? She shook her head, shrugged her shoulders, spread her hands in every gesture she knew to indicate she didn't understand. It was hopeless. She looked at the bleeding leg of Koti. It was still bleeding! He must be alive.

She knelt beside him, holding him, rocking him, examining him. It wasn't as bad as Arturo's leg. He wouldn't need a tourniquet, maybe stitches and antibiotic. *This is the jungle. No doctors. No antibiotics. No needle and thread. He might die from a simple infection made by a stone axe.* Stone. From caveman days. Anakoli must have hit him in the head with his stone axe before Koti had taken out his axe. However it had happened he was unconscious, she tried to wake him, but he didn't stir. What was that lump on his arm? From a poison dart. "Oh no! Don't die on me." She shook her fist at the man, who shook his blowgun at Koti.

She looked about the "encampment" for her pack. She had had it with her in the net. Samal had told her a poisonous dart from the blowgun wouldn't kill, just make a man very sick. Maybe Mamacita's snake anti-venom would help. She saw her pack lying under a tree beyond her reach. Three feet of rope around her ankle was pretty short. *He's treating me like an animal. He doesn't even know whether I'm human or not. I hope he doesn't behead me and shrink my head to carry in his pouch.*

She jumped up, shouting and pointing to herself. "American shaman! Jamie is an American shaman." She walked to the end of the short woven rope and gestured toward her pack. "Bring it to me."

He turned away, not responding—not interested or not caring. She tried again, her fist tapping her chest. "American shaman." She reached for his large pouch. He slapped her hand away, but turned to look at her pack. She nodded vigorously, gesturing again.

Anakoli went to the pack, picked it up, and brought it. She opened the zipper and took out the packets of medicines from Mamacita. Nothing for concussion. Nothing for Koti's leg. Only snake anti-venom which might not work against curare. She opened the bag of flowers, crushed them in her fingers until she felt some juice, and rubbed it on the small dart wound. What would she do if he died? She was alone in the jungle with a primitive wild man. She couldn't talk to him. *Don't panic.* Her mind stopped. *Why not?*

The shaman's brows furrowed under the blue feathers.

Anakoli stooped to rub his hand over the zipper of the pack. He had never seen one! She opened and closed it several times, and let him try it. He actually smiled, though it was hard to tell with the downturned bones in his nose. His fingers ran over the metal rings of her straps. She showed him her packets of medicine, but had no way to communicate what they were for. What she wanted was water to wash Koti's leg wound and his head.

She found her bottle of water, took a swig and offered it to him. He felt the stainless steel in his hands, his eyes round, and handed it back. She took another gulp and offered it again. He put it to his lips and poured some in. After he swallowed he nodded and handed it back. She poured the rest on the leg wound. She took her neck scarf, dirty as it was, to stanch the little bit of bleeding still left and tied it around the leg. She gestured for more water, hoping he would understand.

Anakoli took the bottle and walked over to a small creek. He crossed the creek and picked some leaves of a plant on the other side. He gave her the water and after she washed the leg again he packed the leaves on the wound before she bandaged it with the scarf, and nodded her thanks. Then she cradled Koti's head in her lap and laved his scalp and face. "Wake up, Koti. I need you." It didn't work.

Anakoli glanced at the sky and went back to work on the poles with his stone axe.

Where was Koti's iron axe? He must have dropped it in the fight. *Where's my machete? It was in the net with me.*

She examined the glen they were in. In the daylight she could see that the land and the mass of the jungle trees varied in height. She recognized the ceiba tree rising higher than the rest. Nevertheless, it was dim under the canopy. Here in this glen small trees and bushes with large leaves bent over her. Orange fruits hung from smaller bushes with thin leaves. A few grasses grew along the small stream.

I don't know where I am. Even if I find my machete and escape I don't know which direction to go. We were on the north side of the Tinoca River, and we were walking north to meet Uncle James. I hope he got to the village by now. I hope Tom is with him. What will he do? He was so right. I should have listened. Anyway, I'll have to get back to the Tinoca and follow it east to find the village.

The sky, heavy with rain clouds, gave no hint of the sun to help with direction. This was the dry season? Tears ran down her cheeks again. She wrapped her arms around herself, desperate to live, to be with Tom again, to have someone take care of her. She couldn't do everything herself after all. Independence. Huh.

Anakoli finished his collection of poles and disappeared for a moment. He came back with a stalk of bamboo that he proceeded to shred into thin strips. He tied the poles into a frame with them. He reached under a bush and brought out Jamie's machete. She watched, fascinated by the Indian as he weighed his stone axe in one hand and the machete with his other. He ran his fingers along the edge of the machete and squealed when he cut his fingers. With a glance at her, he disappeared again. She heard chopping noises, and he came back with large palm leaves that he spread over the top of the frame, tying them in place with the bamboo strips.

Just in time. Heavy plops of rain hit her head. Anakoli picked up Koti and laid him gently in the hut out of the rain. By the time he came back for her, streams of water running down the ribs of the heavy leaves overhead had soaked her. Thank god the rain was warm. He did tie her loosely to one of the poles inside. She undid the knot, but what good did it do? Even if she got the machete, lying out of her reach, she couldn't leave. She was better off here. He didn't seem inclined to kill her.

He built a platform about a foot off the ground, stretched his net over it and covered it with leaves. *Oh, good. It will keep us safe from creepy crawlies.*

She took the rope from her ankle and shook it at him. The shaman paid her no attention.

She caught movement in the corner of her eye to her left. Was some animal seeking shelter under the palm leaves? *Don't be silly, Jamie. You're just a bit hysterical.*

Again the movement.

Koti. Anakoli and she both jumped to the unconscious man's side. He groaned and his eyes fluttered open and closed again. She cradled him in her arms. "It's okay, man. You'll be all right. C'mon. Wake up. I expect you'll have a big headache, but you're alive, Koti. Open your eyes again."

Anakoli's brown eyes crinkled when he smiled. Despite that horrid bone in his nose he was glad this man, his enemy, was alive. She couldn't figure it out.

She pulled her pack close and took out her bottle of

aspirin, the only medicine she had carried through the summer. If she put the pills in his mouth, he would choke in this semi-conscious state. She laid them on her pack, pulled the metal ring on the strap around to crush them, and carefully put the powder in her water bottle.

Anakoli watched her intently as she pulled the groaning man up and poured some aspirin into him. He sputtered at first and then swallowed some.

Anakoli pointed at her with his whole hand. "Shaman."

She nodded and poured more aspirin water into Koti.

Anakoli took a half-dozen tan beans out of his pouch and showed her they were all he had. He put them on a flat stone and ground them into a white mash with another stone. He swiftly formed a leaf into a cup, added a bit of rainwater, and offered it to the waking Walaka Indian.

Koti spoke to the shaman in his language and then translated to Spanish for her. "Cupuaçu. Tastes like chocolate. Makes me feel better." He paused to catch his breath and added, "Seeds help with poison from dart. I not die."

"I'm so glad you are alive and awake."

"You all right too. I rest now."

"Can you speak his language? I want to know why he attacked us."

Koti eyed her. He raised his hand to his temple and his eyes crinkled with pain. "If he wants to kill us, we dead last night. You safe. Not die." He stared steadily at the shaman. "But shaman not safe. Maybe he dies. Rest now, talk later." He laid back and closed his eyes.

Jamie rocked back on her heels. Did she hear his words right? The shaman wouldn't kill them? What did he mean the shaman might die? Anakoli didn't know what Koti had said, she was sure.

Anakoli took the pile of wood chips from sharpening the poles, and adding some moss to the pile, twirled a stick in it to make the moss hot enough to catch fire. She had seen someone do that on TV.

How long will it take? Why does he have me here? How long will I be here? Will I die anyway? Clammy sweat rolled over her whole body. She began to tingle all over, like mosquitoes were biting her. She huddled in a corner leaning against the pole. Now was a good time to get out Mamacita's oily mix. She covered her arms and face and exposed legs using most of the oil. Then she shivered and sneezed despite the heat. She hoped she wasn't getting sick. Maybe she just needed some food.

Speaking of food…

Anakoli had actually started a tiny fire. He fed it with some kind of cottony stuff. He walked into the trees again in the rain. Curious and hungry, she followed him. She was soaking wet already anyway. When he saw her he stopped and mumbled what was only gibberish to her ears. Then he leaned down and pointed out a small trail through the brush. They followed it for about fifteen meters, and in the snare at the end of it a guinea pig like animal was chewing on the snare. What was the name of that animal—capybara, she thought. She was not surprised at what happened next.

The shaman twisted the neck after singing words

over it and carried it back to the shelter. He pulled his stone knife from that large pouch to slit it open. Jamie searched the bottom of her bag for the small knife she carried and offered it to him. She was too late, however, because he had already beheaded and gutted the animal. He laid it in the ashes, red-brown skin side down, and she soon smelled the hair burning, while the wisps of smoke rose making the shelter seem almost homey and safe. She grasped how desperate her need was to be safe and cared for.

Anakoli was gathering the orange fruit outside in the rain. He cut the cooked meat into three portions and set one aside for Koti. Jamie brushed as much of the ash as she could off the meat before devouring it quickly, wiping her hands on her pants. The fruit she ate had a citrus taste. She ate the small seeds also when she saw the shaman swallow them.

She finished all that he gave her, and sighed, almost replete. She would survive, if she could find her way back to the river, if it would stop raining, if the shaman didn't change his mind, if a jaguar or a wild boar didn't kill her, if Tom and Uncle James were waiting for her—if, if, if…

Chapter 14

The Shaman

Samal took Tom by the arm. "Do not rush into the jungle. Jamie Patrick will be with her uncle by now. Just wait here. They will arrive soon enough."

Samal's words did not calm Tom. He needed to be sure she was all right. He was responsible for her. His heart pounded with the need to move. "You said that the Sumolu Indians might attack them on the path as they walk here, and they have already been delayed for two extra days because of her uncle's broken ankle. They might be a tempting target. I want to leave now. They can't be too far away, as you say."

"I do not like to go into the jungle. The Sumolu are experts with blowguns. They do not use knives or machetes. They can hide along the trail and attack from a distance. You can't see them. Their darts are poisonous and silent."

Shaken for a moment by the man's fear, Tom hesitated. "You are right. I don't know how to fight Indians with blowguns." The rational part of him understood the wisdom of waiting for her, but his animal instincts were driving him.

"I have a pistol."

Tom stared at the man as the burn spread through him. He pushed Samal out of the way and turned toward the opening in the trees where the path to Jamie started. "I'll go myself. I don't need to wait for you. I don't want any gun." He had walked through the forest in Nicaragua alone. He could do it here for the few hours it might take.

Samal shouted at him. "Wait. Give me five minutes. I will pack some supplies and come with you." He ran into the store.

Tom paced while he waited. He looked over the two canoes by the riverbank. He stared at the bare-breasted women with their children who were staring at him. They wore pink panties and had white spots on their faces. Samal came out with a pack over his shoulder and handed Tom a candy bar and a bottle of water. They moved quickly into the shade over the uneven ground.

The thick pad of leaves concealed many roots and potholes to trip him up, so he soon slowed to an unsteady walk. After a while rain pelted down from the canopy in big drops. Whenever he hit a patch of sunlit area the path got soggy and slippery. He examined carefully where he put his feet, sometimes using the machete to move branches out of the way.

If Indians were watching, or planning to attack, he wouldn't see them.

When two Indians appeared in front of him, he jerked back, tumbling into Samal behind him. Tom pulled himself upright, his arm aching, his chest tight, machete raised and ready. Were they enemies? They were too close to use the blowguns they carried.

Samal pushed around him, brushing leaves out of the way. The Indians stood unmoving, leaning on their blow-guns, and spoke to Samal.

How stupid to assume they were about to attack. I should not get carried away like that. I really don't trust that animal part of me. They must be from the uncle's tribe, the Walaka. What are they talking about so long? He saw the penis cones, the ear bones and the white spots on their cheeks like the women in the village. What did Jamie think of them?

Samal squatted and invited Tom down beside him. "These Indians say that Uncle James is only a small walk away." Tom waited while the man took out his candy bar and began chewing. "It is hard for me to say this," Samal continued. "Jamie is not with her uncle. The Indians said that a net on the path caught someone, and someone else fought the attacker and was bloodied. That is all they know. I told them about Jamie coming out to meet them with Koti, their wise man's son. Now they think that a Sumolu man has stolen them."

Stolen them? Tom froze as it washed through him.

Jamie was gone? His hand trembled like his voice. "Is she dead?"

He waited for the answer, to find out if he was alone.

"No. They are sure of that because they found no body and only a little blood. Besides, she is a woman, not a warrior."

A woman. His woman. Not a warrior. I'm a warrior. I will find her. Strength lifted him. If the Indians knew she was not dead, then she must be alive. Stolen was infinitely better than dead. "We must find her. Tell them, Samal."

He watched the Indians' faces as Samal translated. They seemed uncertain and Samal said they would kill any Sumolu they found, but that they did not want to search for them because then they might kill the whole Sumolu tribe.

"I don't understand." He shook his head, his voice rising. "You are warriors. I am a warrior. Can't you follow the path the Sumolu warrior made through the jungle?"

"Yes, if it doesn't rain, but it rains," they replied through Samal. "We must bring the doctor and his baskets to the village."

Ah, yes. Uncle James with the broken ankle. Uncle James would help. The animal strength roared through Tom. He knew what to do. "We will go to the doctor and bring him to the village. Then we will trail my woman and your wise man's son through the jungle. When we find them, we will kill the Sumolu who took her." A part of him heard his own words and knew he didn't want to kill anyone. He only wanted Jamie.

Samal had a funny look on his face when he translated the Walaka answer. "They say this is good. They will take care of the doctor until the big bird comes to take him away. They will be happy to look for the trail to Jamie. Do not worry about killing the Sumolu. They will die."

Okay. They agreed with the plan. "Let's get moving." Tom gestured the Indians on ahead and they moved swiftly down the path. He only stumbled twice.

ↃↃↃↃ

A bored hopelessness accompanied Jamie as she lay down next to Koti on the sleeping platform. At least she had her pack for a pillow. She removed all of the twigs and leaf ribs she could find to make the leaf pads more comfortable. Still she woke twice to remove another twig that pressed into her bones. Anakoli's coughing kept her awake also. What was the matter with him? Each time she woke, her mind roamed over how she could get away from her captor. Her thoughts kept on in circles, never coming to an end, a hope, a solution.

It was all her fault. She had had to be so independent, show Tom she didn't need him, show her father she wasn't a baby to be coddled and protected to the point of suffocation. *I would sure like a little coddling right now, Tom.* What was he doing? Sleeping in Machazo?

Would Tom ever forgive her for ignoring his pleas to

wait one more day, to keep safe? Yes, he would forgive her. He really loved her. She felt his hands roaming her belly. Would she have another chance to feel that? She ached from sleeping on the platform and not having Tom.

In the dawn light Anakoli disappeared into the jungle again. Maybe he was searching for more food. Maybe he would come back with some more Sumolu. She shivered at the thought. Some of the Amazon tribes had been headhunters she was sure. How did they get those heads to shrink? Probably took the brain out and filled the cavity with sand or salt. *What would I look like all wrinkled and filled with sand...*

A different kind of boredom set in. She really didn't have anything to do. She gathered some of the orange fruit. She picked up all of the dry wood chips she could find and stacked them by the fire. She sat by Koti and washed him. He finally woke, drank some water, and ate some fruit. She admired her own patience. Finally she asked, "Why is he not killing us? After all, we are not Sumolu."

"I do not know the answer. We ask him when he comes back."

"And did you say he might die? Why?"

"I know the answer. Many years ago white man finds Walaka. They take jungle land and cut trees. They kill us, but we kill them. More men come and Walaka die. We get sick and die. We have many people then. Now we have small number."

Uncle James told her the last time she saw him that less than two hundred Walaka remained. "That is terrible.

Really bad. Why do you not hate us, the white people?"

"First years we hate you. Then good people come. They bring iron axes, machetes, and pots. Then your uncle comes. He puts needles in babies. Babies not die. He learns medicine from us, from our plants."

"What about Anakoli?"

"Before white man, we talk to Sumolu. We trade women and food. Now we not want to make Sumolu sick. We only talk across long field. We do not give trade women. They think white man wants to kill them. They right. Some white men bad. They kill trees and we have no more food. We get sick. If we close to Sumolu, they die too."

"You think Anakoli will die because we are here? He cannot get sick from me or you. We are not sick."

"Doctor says he get sick anyway because he not have needle."

He's talking about vaccination and antibiotics. He's probably right. Yesterday I was coughing and sneezing for some reason. Last night and this morning Anakoli coughed without stop. Oh my god...Yesterday morning I passed my water bottle from my mouth to his!

"But, Koti, how could it happen so fast?"

"I do not know. Doctor says it happens. We do not talk with Sumolu so they don't die like Walaka."

"Now I am scared. What will we do if he gets sick and dies? What if he brings other Sumolu here and they kill us? They might die too. The whole tribe might die."

"Yes. We ask him why he wants kill us, but also why he not kill us, if he comes back."

"If? I didn't think of that." She couldn't stand to talk to Koti anymore, so she got up and walked. She came back to him in two minutes and hollered at him. She heard the whine in her voice. "Koti, you have to get better so that we can go back to the river. You have to get better so that we can find some food."

"Head hurts. Hard to breathe because of poison." He grasped his head with both hands and tried to shake the pain out. At least that was what she supposed he was doing. He stopped in a moment. "Okay. I rest, you get food."

She clasped her knees together and rocked back and forth. Could she find some roots that she could dig up or trees with fruits? Bananas maybe? It wouldn't be long before the fruit in the glen was gone. If Anakoli didn't come back tonight with food, she would gather all of the fruit and wake Koti to tell her where to find something edible. Koti could tell her how to make a snare and how to get to the river. If they had one good meal, maybe he would be able to get up and walk. She laughed at her "independence." All people depended on others.

She didn't cry. She sat and stared as various scenarios flashed through her mind. Finally she got up to follow the capybara path into the jungle to look at the snare, but it was gone. She found some red berries, but who knew if they were poisonous. She'd better not eat them. She picked a bunch and carried them back to the camp anyway to ask Koti when he woke up. She kept a small fire going, but the chips would soon be gone.

She hoped Anakoli was not going back to his tribe;

he would make them all sick. If his tribe died, it would be her fault. Genocide. She let her head hang. It was too hard to think about.

She rolled over and tried to take a nap, but her mind wouldn't stop.

What's the matter with me? Why did I refuse to do what Tom asked and stay out of the jungle? I love him and trust him with my life. Did I think Uncle James was more important than Tom? Was I just too damn stubborn to let someone else tell me what to do? It's too late now. I might die. I might be a murderer, even without a gun. Maybe I'm not good enough for Tom. Tom, I love you. I have to get back to you.

It occurred to her that she could make a travois with bamboo poles like Koti's Walaka brothers had made to pull her uncle. She had the machete. She had seen the shaman make the strips to tie the branches of the shelter together. She could do that to make a travois to pull Koti with her to the river. *I can't let him die too. That would be too much.*

She was hacking away at a bamboo stalk when a hand touched her arm. Screaming, she swung the machete around and stopped short when she saw it was Anakoli. She stood with the machete in the air, panting from the fight-for-her-life adrenaline rush. He must have heard her chopping the bamboo.

Anakoli was panting too, covered with sweat, his blue feathers swinging from his ears. The white spots on his cheeks streaked when he wiped at the sweat. He dropped his sack and opened his mouth to speak. He sank to his knees in front of her instead, coughing.

She dropped the machete, put his arm over her shoulders, and dragged him to his feet. "C'mon, man, walk. Back to camp. You can do it. I can't carry you. Stop coughing. Keep moving. It's not far. Just a few more feet." Her knees buckled but she forced them straight and kept going, his heavy body dragging when he couldn't move his feet. He couldn't understand a word she said, but he mumbled answers anyway.

She dragged him under the canopy of palm leaves and laid him alongside Koti, who stirred and woke. "Koti, wake up. I need to talk to Anakoli." Her hand rose to her chest. *Both men sick. My fault. Have to do something.* She powdered some more aspirin and gave it to Anakoli.

He coughed and raised his hand to his throat, with a weak smile under his nose bone. She ran back into the jungle to the bamboo stand and scooped up the machete and the shaman's heavy sack. When she sank to her knees beside the men, Koti opened his eyes.

"Anakoli says he can't breathe. He says you shaman. You cook food. Make him better." Koti stared at her. "You shaman like doctor?"

"No. But do not tell Anakoli." Her eyes slid to the sack, and she pulled it close to examine the contents: a coati, two fish, and three cylindrical pieces of root about a foot long in addition to his various bags of beans and seeds.

Jamie took a deep breath. She was the only one who could do it. She had never gutted an animal before. Her pen knife wouldn't do it. She leaned over the shaman and patted his knife in his jaguar belt. He opened his eyes and handed it to her. He asked something in a raspy voice. Koti translated, "Water."

She took her water bottle and ran back and forth from the stream to the men until they were both satisfied. Koti told her to add more chips to the fire.

Then she took the knife and decided to pretend she was a surgeon who had an operation to do. She would be calm and steady as she operated. It wouldn't be any different than cutting up a piece of meat for dinner. She cut the belly of the coati and opened it as wide as possible. A palm leaf would hold the animal's innards until she could get rid of them. After using the knife to scoop the guts out she cut off the head and the feet. Gagging, she ran to the stream to rinse her hands and the meat until she thought it was good enough. After throwing the coati on the fire hair side down, she operated on the fish. Koti told her to chop slices from the root and throw them in the ashes too. She gathered the orange fruit that Koti called camu camu. One of the big leaves from the glen's brush served as a dinner plate when the coati looked and smelled done.

She fed the three of them one bite at a time. It was a satisfying feast for her and Koti, but Anakoli had trouble getting it down between small breaths. Jamie wrapped the leftovers in a leaf—life was so simple here in the jungle—and sat beside the two men. Koti leaned against a pole between her and the sick shaman. It was time to let her questions out. On the other hand she feared the answers. She wanted to be safe with Tom and tell him how sorry she was for her stubbornness and how she loved him. Rain began to pelt the green roof again and she sat on her pack huddling close to them. Koti's leg warmed her leg on one side, and the shaman's arm warmed her other.

"Koti, would you ask Anakoli some questions for me?" She needed Koti to stay conscious and translate for her. Anakoli was the only one who knew where they were, and how she could get back to Tom and her uncle in Machazo.

He grunted a yes.

Hmmm. "Did he go back to see his tribe today before he came with the food?"

The shaman's eyes widened and he struggled to sit up.

"He says no. Why you ask?"

"Because I am scared that the whole tribe might die."

Koti translated. Anakoli frowned and she heard anger in his long reply.

"You must not curse my people, he says. Why you want curse us? Why Walaka no like us now? Many years no trade, no women. White man tells Walaka no trade. We kill white man so no more curse."

She had not anticipated her shame. Her heart was in her stomach. She stood and stumbled away for a minute, covering her eyes. With a small moan, she beseeched Koti to explain that her people had made the Walaka tribe sick many years ago.

"Many Walaka got sick and died, and now the white shaman, my uncle, uses a needle to save the Walaka babies. Tell him the Walaka do not trade with the Sumolu or give them women because they do not want to make the Sumolu sick."

Anakoli didn't seem to understand, and shook his head weakly.

"'Why trade makes us sick,' he asks. He says he thinks you not bad. Maybe other white people bad."

How to explain her world to this man who knew nothing beyond the jungle? "Tell him that white men make the air bad between people and they get sick. It is not a curse. It is the way the air moves, like water moves from one spot to another."

"I am weak. It is hard to think." He closed his eyes and lay flat.

Jamie took a deep breath and decided to come right out with it. It was the only way to get his help. "I am very sad. I have made the air between us bad and you are sick. Perhaps you will die. You must not go back to your tribe or the bad air from you will kill them." *It's true. I am a killer.*

His eyes flew open again. "You are strong, a woman shaman. You can help me."

"Maybe. I do not have medicine with me. If I can get you to my uncle, who is a very powerful shaman, he can save you with his medicine. You must tell me how to get to the Tinoca River from here. We can follow the river to the place white men come, the village Machazo."

"He wants to help you," Koti translated.

She nodded compulsively and tears welled up. He would help them. Koti would stay conscious so he could translate, even if he couldn't walk. The shaman would stay alive to show her the way. She would get to Tom.

"Koti, why did he capture us?"

That hardly visible smile tugged at Anakoli's mouth again. "I not want to capture you. I want to capture white man shaman. I want to stop curse. Net capture you because you on path, not shaman." His face settled into a frown beneath the blue feathered hair band. "Most important. I want to know how white man work. I want to know how make big loud bird in sky drop ten axes and pots and long knives like your knife." He pointed to her machete. "They fall from sky last year. I not like. Too…sharp for me. Not our way. Some Sumolu want kill animals and men with hard knives, but I no want to kill. I want to know how make hard knives. I come to capture one white man and one Walaka to talk."

He was curious. Moreover, he would help her and Koti. She glanced at Koti who had drifted off again. She wanted to hug both men, but just patted their arms instead. "Stay awake, Koti. Ask the shaman how to get back to Machazo. Do we go to the river?"

"He says you follow the creek to Tinoca River. Find his canoe. Go down the river to the trail where he finds you. Follow the trail return to Machazo. You go now."

"Not yet. I have to make a travois like your brothers made for my uncle. I can drag both of you to the river and we can go in the canoe to my uncle who will have medicine."

"No. Leave us here. A woman not strong to pull travois. I am not die. I am better. Poison not so strong in me now. My head better. Sumolu shaman Anakoli maybe dies. That good."

"I can't just leave you lying here. It's my fault you and Anakoli are sick. A snake might get you or a poison frog. I have to get you to my uncle."

Koti actually laughed. She hadn't heard him laugh before. "You not know my jungle. You go now. Leave some food. In two days I am strong to walk to my village."

"What about Anakoli?"

Koti shrugged. "Maybe he dies."

She turned away from the warrior, glad he would live, but her face warmed in shame to think the shaman would die because he was curious. She didn't want anybody to die because of her, not Julio and not the shaman. If only Tom were here to help her. A moan slipped out. She wiped her forehead and picked up her machete. She would do what she must.

Chapter 15

To the River

Tom knelt beside Uncle James, who rested under a ceiba tree with its tall roots cradling around him. A pale-skinned man in a white long-sleeved shirt, his blond head streaked with gray, he appeared ghost-like compared to the four men and two boys squatting around him. His broken ankle rested at an odd angle. Clearly it needed a cast.

"Are you Tom, Jamie's young man?"

"Yes, her fiancé actually. She—"

"Where is she? She's such a sweetheart. Is she waiting at the village?"

Tom looked at Samal's shocked face and knew that the doctor didn't know Jamie was gone. "Uncle James, Jamie came out to meet you with the Indian Koti. Your Indians say a Sumolu captured her in a net. It must be her. He took Koti too. We have to find where the Sumolu took her."

The doctor's face, already a pasty white, drained. He pushed against the tree roots to get up, wincing with pain. Tom rushed to help him stand. "You are sure? Yes, we will find her. My Indians are good at tracking, but the blasted rain has obliterated the signs by now."

The doctor snapped some questions to the Walaka warriors who began to look abashed and upset, waving the ten-foot blowguns around.

"They don't know where the Sumolu warrior took her and Koti. Apparently, they saw only one set of tracks away from the trail so it is one man who took her and Koti too." Choking on his words, Uncle James added, "She is probably alive."

Probably? My darling—Tom's hand came up with the machete and he slashed at a nearby palm trunk and, with one stroke, sent it crashing to the ground, scattering the Indians around him.

"Careful, laddie. Save that energy for when we find the man who stole her." His slight Irish accent caught Tom's attention. "For sure, he headed toward Sumolu territory," Uncle James continued. "The quickest way to find her is to follow the river southwest into their territory. We have to get to Machazo for the boat. Let's go." He lowered himself to the travois, careful not to put weight on the ankle that stuck out.

Tom took the lower end of the travois, holding the doctor's weight, and they navigated the trail quickly through the failing evening light. He didn't like feeling as if he were heading in the wrong direction, away from her.

It was even worse when he found out they could not leave in the rusty old *Saviour* until morning. Uncle James explained it clearly, though. "The water in the Tinoca is tea-colored because it has so much wood in it. Because of the plethora of logs we have to go slowly around them in a boat with a propeller. We have to see the logs in the water. The Indians will go ahead of us upstream in the canoes. Do not worry, laddie, it will be faster than walking."

They ate dinner with everyone in the village around a campfire. The black gallinaceous chicken was fine, as well as a greens and beans mixture cooked in a pot. Tom rose to walk impatiently several times. He could not relax, wondering where she was, how the Sumolu was treating her, and if she would forgive him for letting her go. *As if I had a choice. She is so independent and doesn't even know it. I hope I can forgive myself.*

While they sat by the fire, Uncle James all of a sudden threw his chicken down and asked one of the men a question. Tom asked him why the men were so loud when they answered him.

"Whew. It occurred to me that it might have been someone from the Kikiti tribe farther south. They are head hunters. My Walaka men insisted that it was a Sumolu warrior because they found a blue macaw feather on the ground where the attacker accosted Jamie. I am relieved. The Sumolu aren't that bad. As I understand it, they aren't cannibals anymore, at least in the dry season, which it is right now."

Tom spit out a "But—" before the talkative man continued.

"In the dry season it rains only half the time. In the rainy season it rains every day and the hunting is bad. The river basins all flood. That's when the Sumolu might be tempted."

Tom shrank back and threw the remainder of his chicken in the fire. He wandered toward the dark forest with his stomach roiling. Behind a bush, he vomited. After a few deep breaths, he headed back to the fire. He would not let it end this way.

౪౩౪౩

I will not let it end this way, Jamie thought. For the third time, she retied the two poles of the travois. She had tied the net between the two poles at one end and rolled the feverish shaman off the sleeping platform an hour ago. He had leaned on it, semiconscious, until she had maneuvered the weak man to the side of the travois and pushed him over onto the net. When she tried to pull them, the rope she had fashioned with Koti's directions slipped off the ends of the poles. "Damn!"

Koti rolled off the platform, losing his breath as he hit the ground. After a minute, he looked at the travois. "Tie a piece of bamboo pole between the ends of the long poles, where the net is. Poke holes in all the poles with your knife. Tie the poles together with the cords going through the holes. They will not come apart."

It took a half hour to poke the holes and tie them

with the strips she had taken from the bed platform. Koti had been vertical for a few moments before he climbed back on the remaining platform. How could she leave him? He was better, though. She had to believe every word that came out of his mouth. She would not be able to take both men.

She tried pulling the travois with the weight of Anakoli on it on the level ground under the shelter. It was hard, but she could do it, even with her pack on her back. She took the leftover food pack from the corner under the ceiling and divided it in half. It would be enough for Koti for two days. She wasn't sure how much she would need.

She rolled the groaning shaman off the net, padded it with leaves, and rolled him back. "Anakoli, pay attention to me." She held him in her arms. "You have to stay awake enough to tell me how to get to the river. How long will it take?" Koti translated for her. The shaman focused his eyes for a minute.

"Only until the sun gets high in the sky. Not all day. Guarana beans for your strength in his pouch."

She washed the fiery forehead of the shaman and fed him the final bit of aspirin. She changed the leaves on Koti's cut leg and gave him water and camu camu. After enjoying the citrus fruit for the last time, she looked at the sky dotted with white bits of clouds over the mountains, and whispered her many thanks to the warrior. "We will meet again, wise son of the wise man."

Koti smiled and then snored.

After stuffing Anakoli's blowgun through the loops of the net, she picked up her backpack, tied the bag of food to it, filled her water bottle, and lifted the end of the travois. With a big hitch, she pulled it steadily over to the creek and dragged it through the grasses at the edge. Then she came to the end of the glen.

Large bushes lined the edge of the water, interrupted by small trees. Jamie stopped. *This will be hard. Can I do it? Only one way.* She pulled the machete from her belt and felt the edge as the shaman had done. With a deep breath, she stepped forward and leaned to swipe at the branches close to the ground. Heavy leaves fell in front of her. *Not so bad.*

She stepped forward again along the creek and began swiping steadily. Ten minutes of chopping cleared about ten feet and then she had to catch her breath. A small tree, too big to cut easily with the machete, barred her way. Should she drag the shaman through the water, or make the path around the tree? The cool water of the spring might help the poor man's fever, but too many stones in the water would make the traverse impossibly uncomfortable for him. Around the tree it was. Rested enough, she went back to work.

She kept an eye on her watch, thinking about how Anakoli had ignored it. After a half hour of steady hacking, she threw down the machete triumphantly. Her arm was a bit shaky, but she was satisfied with a hundred yards of cleared path along the bank. It was time to pull the travois this distance before she began again. Her arm needed the pause.

The shaman had rolled off the travois while she had worked, and was tossing and turning on the ground. After a long drink for herself she poured a bottle full of water on him and rolled him back onto the net as gently as she could. She took her belt off and threaded it through the net to hold him tightly on it. With both hands, she got a good hold on the travois and tugged it along the stream. It moved fairly quickly, even if it wasn't as smooth as she anticipated. From moment to moment, she would have to give it an extra tug over some unseen root.

Happy with her progress, she let her mind wander to how it would be when she reached Machazo. Tom was waiting, she was sure. His arms around her would solve everything. *I'm so sorry, Tom. I should have listened to you. Why am I so pig-headed? Uncle James is important, but not as important as you. How's your arm? Does it hurt? I'm coming, Tom. I'm coming. My arm hurts too.*

She straightened her aching back and took a look at how she was doing. Each half hour stretch of chopping seemed to be bringing her a shorter distance cleared. She was getting a blister on her thumb. She tore a strip from the bottom of one of her tee shirts and wrapped it. If it got too bloody and sore she might be tempted to give up. As it was, every swipe hurt now. Nevertheless, she had to keep on. She had to get to the river and find the canoe before dark. Glancing at the sky, she hurried herself back to work. No signs of rain today. On the other hand, rain would sure feel good. She wiped her forehead and swung the machete again.

Anakoli was inert on the net. *I want him to live. He will live. So will I.* She pulled the bamboo poles and struggled down the bank of the stream toward the river.

She hoped she would have no trouble finding the canoe when she got there. She wondered how far it was now. The sun was getting lower in the sky.

She gave a hard tug to get the net over a stubborn root. She heard a crack and fell to her knees as the tied ends separated. Ouch! A two inch sharp thorn scratched her and made her bleed. She hoped it wasn't poisonous. She wiped it peremptorily on her pants and examined the broken travois. Could she get Anakoli up to lean on her shoulder? She could maybe walk him the rest of the way. No. He was too sick. So fast, but it had happened.

The hole in the left pole that she had made with the pen knife had rasped at the bamboo strips that had tied it to the other pole and had torn. Done. Kaput. She had no time to make more. Besides, she could see no stand of bamboo handy. A piece of a vine? No, it wouldn't be strong enough. Ah! She unbelted the shaman and threaded the belt through the holes.

She tried to wake the shaman, but he just mumbled. A vine would hold him to the net. Five minutes later it was done. How could anyone live without a machete? She laughed at herself, appreciating the pause for repair. She wiped the blood off her arm in the brook and ignored the exhaustion encouraging her arms to hang, encouraging her to sit down and take a nap. A few bites of cold fish from the bag helped.

The creek widened into a sunny area, and the current slowed, with grasses growing in the water and sticks almost damming it up in places. She heard frogs and knew they might be poisonous. Insects flew into her face and mouth. How could she follow the stream if it turned into a swamp? The travois sank into mud for a short way

The sun approached the trees in the west. This was the tropics, practically on the equator. It only took ten minutes for it to get dark in this part of the world. She struggled on, pulling the heavy shaman over the roots, cut some more, pulled again. She hurt, but couldn't stop. A few more steps and she spotted a sandy stretch in the river. Without hesitation she dragged the poles by the belt into the stream. Fish brushed against her, but she didn't stop. It seemed to be widening a bit.

Then she began to hear the low sigh, the mutter of the river water, complaining between the banks. That was the way she felt. Around a few more curves and as the sun began to dip below the trees, she saw the tea- colored twenty-foot-wide river absorbing the clear water under her feet. She dropped the poles and staggered to the edge of the Tinoca River. She had to find the canoe before it got dark.

She stumbled over it. It lay at the side of the river in mud of the same color. Okay. She only had to climb into the canoe and float down to the village. She was too tired to focus on how to steer the canoe, too tired to make a platform to sleep on.

A large tree with a four foot wide trunk rose high on the bank above her. Underneath the tree the roots spread out leaving a small recess underneath. It looked comfortable and safe.

She pulled the travois beside the canoe, untied the shaman, and woke him enough to pull him under the miniscule shelter. With her head on her backpack and her arms around a shaking Anakoli, she fell asleep.

Chapter 16

Jaguar

She woke with a sudden panic about snakes. Useless. It was definitely too late to worry about that. Today she would go down the river to Tom. She scratched her nose, itchy from the shaman's feathers brushing her face. The sun hinted at morning light.

Ravenous, she reached for her sack of cooked food. A snarl made her jump. It came from the bushes to her left. She tried to crawl back, but the shaman was in her lap and the roots of the big tree behind her. The snarl repeated and she saw the gleam of eyes in the dark under the bush. A small scream escaped her. She pushed the shaman aside and looked for something to throw at the animal. She found her hairbrush in her pack and threw it hard at the bush.

The orange and black of a jaguar burst from the bush and streaked toward her. She instinctively pulled her pack in front of her, shrieking at the top of her lungs. The jaguar stopped about ten feet from her, his paws clenching and unclenching, his tail switching. His eyes stayed on her and his snarl was a steady rasp.

No! She grabbed a sandal and threw it. "Go away!"

The jaguar commenced to pace back and forth, as if planning a rush. What was this cat doing attacking her in the daytime? Jaguars hunted at night. Why was this one here? Was this its den? She took out the other sandal and got ready to fend it off with the machete in the other hand. She wrapped her remaining clothes around her neck. That's what he would try to do, close his teeth on her neck.

The jaguar made a brief dash toward her and then backed off, turning away and turning toward her again. She hit it in the hindquarters with the other sandal as it turned away, forcing it to turn and come even closer as it seemed to conquer its own fear. Now she had nothing to throw.

Sweat covered her as she shook the machete and shouted threats. "Get out of here, you vicious devil. If you come closer I'll tear you limb from limb. I'm bigger than you. I'm human and you're not. Bet you're more afraid than me. Come any closer and I will kill you with my knife."

A vision of Anakoli disemboweling the capybara made her reach for the stone knife tucked into his brown pelt.

She stood up, bent over under the roots, waving the two knives, one stone and one steel. She took a step forward, hollering as menacingly as she could. She blinked and wiped the wetness burning her eyes with her arm. At this, the cat retreated a foot, muscles rippling under the beautiful skin, showing white teeth and fangs.

It didn't run away. She ran out of words and collapsed. She would fight, but the cat was going to tear chunks out of her and shred her skin. *I'll die in the jungle without Tom.*

☙❧

Tom was still tired. All night lying on a root did not help his arm feel any better. The whole day yesterday on the rickety one-engine motorboat had made him miserable with inactivity, while the Walaka Indians surrounding the boat had jumped in and out of their canoes checking out each stream that flowed into the river. The Sumolu had to camp near one of these streams for water. The one pair of footprints walking from Jamie's abduction spot indicated that the warrior had literally carried off both of them. With a heavy load like that, they couldn't be far.

Samal insisted he stay in the boat. "You do not know about the curare of the Sumolu blowguns. It might be stronger than Walaka curare."

I won't stay in the boat today. Too much time to think about cannibals. He rolled out of the blanket Samal had sold him, and peed in the river. Others stirred also as the sky lightened. He heard a monkey screech.

Samal sat up when a Walaka shook him. He waved his arm, pointing upstream with his whole hand, talking very fast. Samal leaped up. "That's a human scream!" He pushed Tom toward *The Saviour*.

If that was her—

He charged for the boat, pushed Samal aside, and vaulted over the rail to reach the wheel. He turned the key and pulled out as Samal clambered over the edge. The men in the canoes could not pull ahead fast enough and dragged behind. At full speed, he still had to steer between the floating trees. Samal leaned forward warning him when he saw signs of submerged trunks. He did bump one that skewed the boat sideways as he made the next turn.

More screams, and then he heard Jamie's voice shouting. She wasn't dead yet! The Indians behind him warbled high-pitched bays.

Samal shook him and pointed to something on the bank beyond where a stream entered. "Sumolu canoe."

"Where?" His gaze darted upstream and along the river banks, as he slowed the boat. A framework lay in the mud.

"Is that a motor? Help! Help me!" he heard her shout. She was up under the big tree.

"I'm coming," he called, pushing Samal aside and jumping into the water.

"Is that you Tom? Look out! There's a jaguar in the bushes in front of me."

He hit the river bank running. *There's a jaguar in me.* He paused, searching, and smelled the musky cat before he saw it about two feet in front of him. The snarl grew to a grumble and the head swung back and forth between him and Jamie, deciding which way to spring.

Jamie froze above him.

Tom's fingers twitched. Unthinking, he leaped. He caught the hind paw as the jaguar turned on him lightning fast, teeth closing on his left wrist. Tom tightened his grip on the paw despite the distant pain. His balled right fist hammered on the head and the teeth loosened. With both hands, he clutched the whiskered cheeks of the cat, falling on top of it. The hind claws scraped repeatedly at his belly, but he didn't let go. A gunshot went off over his head. He and the cat rolled over and over together. Jamie and the others were shouting as if at a distance. He felt a stone under him and twisted to the side as he rolled to his knees, staring into green eyes and gaping teeth gripped in front of him. The cat twisted to get away, but Tom lifted the weight of its body and smashed the head down on the stone. Another fierce smash and the animal stilled.

He stared at the cat's head, unbelieving, not letting loose, and smashed it one more time.

The jabbering Indians came up beside him and gently pried his fingers off the beautiful body. Jamie was all over him, kissing him, crying as he held her. The blood on his ripped shirt seeped all over her and she tore it off to examine his belly and screamed again.

She was hollering at Samal to tell the Indians to get some leaves to pack his wounds. He looked down at his belly and admitted it looked pretty bad. No guts were spouting from it that he could see. He'd be all right until the shock wore off and the pain began.

They led him to the boat. Jamie directed them to the

sick man she had been pulling on a makeshift travois. They placed him in the boat as well. Jamie climbed in beside Tom and held him as the boat raced downriver.

Words bubbled from Jamie as he lay in the comfort of her arms. "I'm so sorry, Tom. It's all my fault. I never should have come into the jungle without you. You are my rock, my man. You are so brave. I will listen to you. I promise."

Her voice droned on. Satisfied they were both safe, he let himself drift off.

Chapter 17

Fiesta

The next day, Tom sat outside on the green plastic chair in the open space in the middle of Machazo. The small village swarmed with people—a lot of modest women in pink panties and proud men in penis cones and feathers. He wanted to walk around too, but the stitches in his belly pulled too much.

Jamie sat on a log beside him, surrounded by a half dozen girls. Samal squatted next to her translating their questions. She wore a necklace of bones sewn onto leather in a striped pattern, a gift from the women. He liked it on her new pink tee shirt. Was she wearing pink panties underneath?

He reached over to rest his good arm on her shoulder, grunting at the pain from shifting, happy to have his woman by his side. "Jamie, what time is the helicopter coming?"

"About noon tomorrow. We'll leave after the fiesta in the afternoon."

"Is Uncle James ready to go?"

"Well, the helicopter pilot will be bringing plaster for a cast to make him more comfortable." She put her warm little hand in his. "I'm so glad he was able to ignore the pain long enough to sew you together. He's anxious to get you to Quito to get some blood into you. He says you will feel fine with a couple of pints. He's pretty good with the needle and thread, but he has no blood here in the jungle."

The memory rose of lying on a pallet in the store with the ghost of a doctor leaning over him, Jamie on one side and Samal on the other for support. In his Irish accent, the doctor had told him, "Hang in there, laddie. A few pricks of Novocain and then we'll sew you up."

Tom wanted to tell Jamie about the jaguar fight, about what had gone on in his head, but "no rush" as his father would say. They had a lifetime to talk about it. She was so absorbed with the kids.

She told the children about airplanes and rockets to the moon, and that the Earth was a ball going around the sun.

"We know that," they chorused. "The doctor shaman told us."

Jamie took out her newly charged cell and started taking pictures. Anakoli came out of the store where he had been exploring. His fascination turned to the phone when he saw the photos. Uneasily, he asked Samal if the photos were a curse. Samal and the children both laughed at his ignorance. A shot of penicillin had swiftly brought him back from his fever, and only a cough remained. He and Uncle James had spent hours yesterday evening talking. The man was really curious about the world, especially about metal and motors. Samal had asked him to help in the store so he could begin to comprehend steel and electricity and the unbelievable number and variety of people in the world. He was coming to accept that he couldn't go back to his tribe.

Tom studied the shaman, intent on learning to take pictures with a phone. He seemed so innocent. No visible hint of cannibalism showed.

I know his instincts to survive are still in there. He could turn violent if he needed to, like me, and every other human on earth. I don't have to worry anymore about what I might do. I'm normal. I protected Jamie.

Jamie was playing tag with the girls now, her raven hair whipping around that pink tee shirt. He felt himself stirring with a hunger for her body. Soon…Soon.

He shuffled in his chair and stood. He'd been sitting still too long. The stitches pulled, but he walked over to the green cave that opened into the jungle path. All the dangers in there, he thought, both real and imagined. Jamie came up beside him, panting a little from running. She hung on his right arm.

He brushed his lips through her hair. "The jungle is like the world opening before us, isn't it? We don't know what's coming next." Her blue eyes shone in her flushed face. He gave her a light kiss. "Wherever you go, wild woman, I'll follow. I promise to ask what you're doing."

She leaned into him, her eyes on the jungle path. "Parts of life are scary. I'll need you to navigate."

⌘

The next morning the air was rumbling with drums. The whole Walaka tribe had arrived for the ceremonies. They had brought a slew of animals to roast, and Jamie ran with the women from fire pit to fire pit checking on the cooking of the armadillos, turtles, raccoon-like coatis, and two tapirs with their prehensile snouts. At least that's what Uncle James had called them. This was the big protein bash for the year. When the "dry" season was over and the floods began, protein would be scarce. She thought they all looked healthy enough. Probably from all the vegetables and fruit they ate. Today they would have manioc, green plantains, and golden papayas with honey. Her mouth watered.

Tom was over by the river, surrounded by young men who wanted to teach him how to use a blowgun. They pantomimed taking a deep breath from the abdomen up. Tom tried, but stopped, clutching his stomach. It was still hard for him to stand up, let alone take a deep breath. Bandages wrapped his arm from shoulder to wrist. She chuckled when he picked up the blowgun. He was going to try it anyway. That was her Tom. She was so proud of him. He was strong in so many ways. She couldn't wait to tell her father what a good choice he had made to send him with her for the summer. She watched Tom flex the muscles of his right arm and pull himself up tall. The young men jabbered and demonstrated. The dart was already in the gun. Had it been dipped in curare? Probably not. The stuff took so long to make, and this was just target practice.

Tom forced that big breath from his abdomen, ignoring the pain, and blew. It must have worked because the young men all raced to the target and triumphantly drew a dart from it. Tom had a silly grin on his face.

A voice spoke over her shoulder. "He good man, strong warrior."

"Koti. You made it back here. I'm so glad you are strong too." She hugged him and then held him at arm's length. She tentatively reached up to his scalp. "How is your head?"

He took her hand down. "Hurts a little. Thank you. You are a good shaman, like the doctor."

She felt herself blushing and looking down. "I am not a shaman."

"Yes. You will see." He left, not limping at all. All the injuries that people had received because of her. *Well, I will do something about it. I will tell Tom I'm going to med school to be a real shaman like my dad and my uncle. I think he will like that. I will definitely listen if he has any objections. I don't want to lose him. What is he going to choose for grad school?* He looked so happy with himself. She loved him that way. She left the fire pit and went over to ask him what he was going to study next year.

His arm went around her comfortably. "Grad school?"

She felt so protected.

"What would you think, darling, if I asked your father to recommend me for the Virginia State med school?"

"I think we will be in the same classes," she told him, squeezing his good arm, with little arrows of delight in her brain. *He asked me what I thought!* "We're two silly fools in love, aren't we?" She was about to kiss him in front of everybody when Uncle James took her elbow.

"Why look at you, Uncle, with a clean white shirt. Who made that crutch for you?"

"Samal. With a make shift crutch to go with my make shift cast I'll be able to make it to the hospital in Quito. Come, lassie. The ceremony is about to start."

Indeed, she hadn't noticed the drumming had increased.

"You too, Tom."

The wise man, Chimbi, stood on a box from the store and spoke, the numerous feathers on his headdress and belt and penis cone waving in bright red as he swung his arms. The red streaks on his chest alternated with purple. With the purple streaks on his face between the white spots he looked rather like the masks the women had made. He stamped his blowgun on the box to make a hollow sound and gestured to two young men to escort Tom to the front to stand on the other box near him. The two warriors came and took Tom's hand out of hers and marched him toward the chief. *What's happening?* She raised her arm toward him. He jerked free of the two men who were smiling and nodding at him, gesturing him ahead. He turned back to Jamie. "Don't worry, kitten. I'll be fine. Trust me." He pinched her cheek gently and walked away with his friends.

Jamie glanced at her uncle, and he patted her hand that was through his arm. "I'll translate for you, lassie."

They took off Tom's brand new tee shirt. His stomach bandage showed above his shorts. His injured arm hung at his side. At least his black eye had faded.

"The wise man says that Tom is a great warrior because he fought the jaguar."

Everybody roared and pounded the blowguns in the ground. They painted two purple streaks on his chest. She squealed in delight. It must be an honor.

The wise man spoke again. "He fought the jaguar with his bare hands, with no machete."

Another roar came from the crowd, and they painted two more purple streaks on his chest.

The wise man spoke a third time. "Samal shot the pistol in the air to frighten the cat away, but the cat was brave also and inflicted wounds on this man. The wounds did not stop him. He fought until he conquered the cat with his bare hands. A true warrior will give honor to the jaguar by wearing the pelt he has won." As the crowd roared again they tied his jaguar pelt to his waist while he stood wide-legged and tall.

Her man had conquered his world. She stomped her feet and hollered with everyone else.

Tom's brow cleared now, but Chimbi had not finished. "As a great warrior who has defended our people, he is now a member of our tribe." They painted white spots on his face and made him stay on the box, arms akimbo, hands on his waist.

The wise man stepped down, and the tribal shaman took his place. Uncle James hopped forward with the crutch under his left arm pulling Jamie with him. They put another box next to Tom's and put Jamie on it. She was so nervous she thought she might faint until she felt Tom's hand reaching over to steady her. She decided to enjoy it. They would have to take her new necklace off if they wanted to take her tee shirt off. She could probably handle it.

The shaman raised his hand. "This woman has used her knowledge and power to save our Koti, to save the shaman from the Sumolu, and to save our whole tribe from the threat of death from the Sumolu because we have such a powerful white man shaman. Her strength is now ours, and our strength is hers."

They put a brown pelt, decorated with teeth like the necklace, around her waist. The crowd roared again. The shaman patted the skin and Uncle James translated. "This is a pelt made from the skin and teeth of a wild boar, known for its wisdom and its strength. You are a strong and wise shaman."

More cheers. Jamie guessed what was coming next when they approached with the pot of white paint. She giggled when they painted white spots on her cheeks.

"Hold still, lassie," Uncle James called.

After a final roar people dragged Tom and her from the boxes and began a ceremonial dance in a circle. The men donned the masks the women had made, including

Tom. She was a woman, and very happy she didn't have to wear a mask. Thrust into the circle by the crowd, Tom and she danced with them, holding hands in the slow shuffle in time with the drums. After several rounds, Uncle James rescued them in a turnabout.

"The helicopter is loaded. Are you ready to leave the jungle?"

"Yes. Yes. Yes."

Jamie looked at Tom. "Do you think they'll let us into a hotel dressed this way?"

The End.

About the Author

Carol J. Megge graduated with an MLA degree from Valparaiso University in Indiana a long time ago. After a career as a teacher of French, Japanese, and English, she has been an inveterate traveler and a novice writer. Having enjoyed three month stays in Turkey, France, and Japan, and visits to China and Egypt, she has stories to tell. Passion and curiosity have been her occasional downfall, as well the prod to make her a writer. Her stories are romances in the widest sense of the word. The risks of adventurous fights against man and nature permeate her novels and these are the situations that make her characters grow.

Megge learned the basics of writing from reading and from other published writers, such as those in her local chapter of Romance Writers of America, and the Florida Chapter of the Historical Novel Society. Her writer friends have mentored, coddled and encouraged her. She loves trying to pass on the wisdom of her age to whomever might take it. She welcomes your thoughts whether deep or shallow at her website, Writers and World Views.